Katha Urdu Library

Sylvat Aziz 1997

'Muqqadiman'

Sylvat Aziz 1997

'Muqqadiman'

MAPPING MEMORIES

URDU STORIES FROM INDIA AND PAKISTAN

Edited by Sukrita Paul Kumar and Muhammadali Siddiqui

KATHA

First published by Katha in 1998

Copyright © Katha, 1998

Copyright © for the original stories held by the authors.

Copyright © for the English translations rests with KATHA.

KATHA
A3, Sarvodaya Enclave
Sri Aurobindo Marg, New Delhi 110 017
Phone: (91-11) 4141 6600, 4141 6610
Fax: (91-11) 2651 4373
E-mail: marketing@katha.org
Website: http://www.katha.org

KATHA is a registered nonprofit organization
devoted to enhancing the joy of reading.
KATHA VILASAM is its story research and resource centre.

General Series Editor: Geeta Dharmarajan
Art Director: Arvinder Chawla
Art Consultant: Pooja Sood
Cover Design: Roma Sinai Mukherji
Production-in-charge: S Ganeshan
Slides of paintings used in the book: Courtesy, Eicher Gallery

Typeset in 10 on 15pt Calisto MT by Suresh Sharma at Katha

Katha regularly plants trees to replace the wood used in the making of its books.

ISBN 978-81-85586-76-2

First Reprint 2012, Second Reprint 2016

☞ CONTENT ☜

ACKNOWLEDGMENTS

PREFACE BY SUKRITA PAUL KUMAR

INTRODUCTION BY MUHAMMAD ALI SIDDIQUI

THE MAN HANGING AT THE CHAURAHA   19

• Anwar Qamar

translated by Rashmi Govind

THE SON'S LETTER   27

• Bano Qudsia

translated by Tahira Khan

THE COW   45

• Enver Sajjad

translated by Shobhana Bhattacharji

REMAINS OF DESIRE   53

• Farkhanda Lodhi

translated by Neshat Quaiser

THE SETTING SUN   73

• Gyas Ahmed Gaddi

translated by Krishna Paul

THE PALE DOG   87

• Intizar Husain

translated by Neshat Quaiser

JOY   109

• Jeelani Bano

translated by Naghma Zafir

KHODU BABA'S TOMB   121
- Joginder Paul

translated by Gillian Wright

FIREFLIES IN A CLENCHED FIST   149
- Mohammad Mansha Yad

translated by Rashid

HONOUR   159
- Qurratulain Hyder

translated by the author

THE UNIT   175
- Salim Agha Qazilbash

translated by Atanu Bhattacharya

BIJOOKA   183
- Surendra Prakash

translated by Sara Rai

AADMI   193
- Syed Muhammad Ashraf

translated by Saleem Kidwai

THE LAST STATION   205
- Umrao Tariq

translated by Anupama Prabhala Kapse & P L Narasimham

MIRAGE ON WATERS   213
- Zaheda Hina

translated by Rashmi Govind and Ayesha Sultana

THE TRANSLATORS
THE EDITORS
THE ARTISTS
ABOUT KATHA

PREFACE

For centuries in the subcontinent, Urdu has been chiselled and polished as a language for fine aesthetic articulation of the human spirit. A rich stream of Indo-Gangetic culture flows within it. Fiction, I believe, is a living document of life in its totality, as also in its specific circumstance in history.

Urdu is traditionally known for its shairi. Lines from Ghalib, Iqbal, Firaq or Faiz are enjoyed by a large number of people who don't read Urdu. But little do people outside the Urdu world know of the highly developed art of the short story in this language. In both Pakistan and India, writers in Urdu have created a very significant and vibrant body of short fiction during the last fifty years. This is really a continuation of the tradition handed down from the pre-Partition times. Strands of Hindu, Buddhist and Persian tradition pooled themselves into dastangoi, the Indo-Persian art of storytelling, which, flowing down to the present times, interacted with western cultures and gradually evolved into jadeed afsana or the modern short story.

On both sides of the border, literature in Urdu has prospered through the extensive publication of journals and books. But unfortunately, there has not been a very easy exchange of these materials due to the intermittent political tensions. It was in this context that Kamleshwar, the eminent writer in Hindi, said so succinctly: "But how can we have a political division of Urdu!" In weaving the story, the writer so naturally pulls the warp from Sialkot or Rawalpindi when the weft may be from Lucknow or Jharia.

These short stories from India and Pakistan capture vital flashes of the human predicament in the subcontinent. The immediacy with which the narration affects the reader's mind speaks for the stark authenticity of the experience presented. While they are all deeply rooted in their specific socio-cultural contexts, the spirit of these stories transcends to a realm where human connections are easily perceived.

Both in the fabulist form and mythopoetic content, Intizar Husain's "The Pale Dog," Surendra Prakash's "Bijooka" or Joginder Paul's "Khodu Baba's Tomb" directly tell the tale of the shared cultures nourished by India and Pakistan. They could have been written by writers of only India or Pakistan; not by a writer from, say, Latin America or from even closer home, Sri Lanka. Again, Zaheda Hina's story "Mirage on Waters," Farkhanda Lodhi's "Remains of Desire" and Qurratulain Hyder's "Honour," delve into gender orientations specific to our societies. They invoke a rethinking of stereotypical ideas about female beauty, the cherishing of female honour in the new world and the quest of woman in changing man-woman relationships.

In Mansha Yad's "Fireflies in a Clenched Fist," the urban woman reacts existentially to the staleness of her routine life in a metropolis. Such an alert temper finds its match in the absurd fate of the incarcerated man in Salim Agha Qazilbash's "The Unit." The man has to choose his own punishment for a crime he did not commit. Another story told with a deep contemporary awareness, "The Man Hanging at the Chauraha" by Anwar Qamar, clutches the reader in its nightmarish captivity. In Syed Mohammad Ashraf's "Aadmi," the man becomes a prisoner of fear, not of animals, but of man. On the other hand, interestingly, Umrao Tariq's "The Last Station" accords a frightening freedom to people in being fugitives, perhaps for ever.

Enver Sajjad's "The Cow" and Jeelani Bano's "Joy" are well-known stories. They offer delicate glimpses of diminishing compassion in modern living. A quiet message lies woven in the narrative of Bano Qudsia's story "The Son's Letter." The solitary old man in the story marries his maid - life moves on. While Gyas Ahmed Gaddi's story "The Setting Sun" etches an unforgettable portrait of Raffu, a boy poised like an eagle for take-off.

Through diverse styles ranging from the folk to the abstract, from the realistic to the symbolic and the absurd, the stories in this selection reveal varied dimensions of life in India and Pakistan. This collage presents harmony in the contrast as much as in the similarity of colours. All borders and barriers are obliterated when, with gusto and rigour, the creative energy takes over.

The translators and editors of this volume have laboured with love and determination to keep the translations as close to the original as possible. I feel indebted to them. We hope that these stories offer a fulfilling experience to the reader.

New Delhi, March   Sukrita Paul Kumar

INTRODUCTION

The Urdu language and its literature have grown from the ground realities of the Indian subcontinent. A glance at the history of this language will show how Urdu fiction represents a cultural heritage shared by India and Pakistan. Urdu belongs to the Shora Saini Prakrit branch of the Aryan language. Both Urdu and Hindi are the products of an area where Braj Bhasha is spoken. In its formative years, Urdu was definitely influenced by the lingual and cultural strains of Sindh and South-West Punjab; however, its origin can be traced to Khadi Boli.

While one can discern its roots in the 12th century poetry of Sindhi, Saraiki and Punjabi, it actually emerges as the language of the Sufi saints in the 13th century. The Sufi saint Baba Farid Ganj Shakar, who is better known as Baba Farid (1186-1265) is credited with being the first Urdu poet. After Baba Farid, Amir Khusro (1208835) appeared as a bright star on the horizon of that poetry where there was a confluence of Hindu-Muslim culture. Some consider Khusro to be the first Urdu poet. The multifaceted genius of Khusro is evident in geet, lyric, rang, songs of celebration, dohe, couplets and pahelis or riddles.

Amir Khusro, followed by Kabir Das and Guru Nanak Dev, demonstrate in their language a strong bonding with Urdu. In fact, even Tulsidas, who was a Hindi poet during the Mughal period, can be placed in the Urdu poetic tradition. Pandit Chandra Bhan Brahman (1575-1662) preceded Muhammad Afzal Meerathi, Abdul Quadir Bedil, Shah,Imad Qualandar, Meer Jafer Zatalli and Khwaja Amani. This led to the era of Wali Dakkani, the father of the Urdu Ghazal.

Early eighteenth century Urdu prose comprised of religious texts and narrative legends. The indulgence in legendary narratives came to a halt after Fasana-e-Aazad when Sir Syed Ahmed Khan, Deputy Nazeer Ahmad and Shibli stepped in with their own distinct prose style. The romantic movement in Urdu, specially in the short stories of Sajjad Haider Yaldram, was a reaction to the dry prose style of Sir Syed Ahmed and his contemporaries. In the short stories and novels of Raashid-ul-Khairi there seems to be an extension of the tradition established by Deputy Nazeer Ahmed. Sir Syed Ahmed Khan's prose style later found itself prospering in the lucidity of Munshi Premchand.

By the latter half of the eighteenth and early nineteenth centuries, British and European poets were reciting English poetry in Indian courts. The spread of English education by European missionaries exposed people to the popular English literary genres of fiction and the short story. This renewed interest in traditional folk forms of narration. To represent a specific reality of human life, the short story became for Urdu writers a favourite form of creative expression.

In the latter half of the century during 1880-81, it was realized that 81% of the owners of magazines and newspapers in Urdu were Hindus. Arya Samajis like Swami Dayanand were getting the 'Yajurveda' translated into Urdu. The ongoing debate between the supporters of the Arya Samaj and its detractors was also being conducted in Urdu. It was in the first decade of the 20th century that a school master from rural Uttar Pradesh, who used the pseudonym Premchand, laid the foundations of Urdu fiction. In the Punjab, Sudarshan busied himself portraying both rural and urban life in his short stories. This was an age when Bengal's literature, and other related fine arts like music and painting were going through the stage of cultural exchange between India and the West. This process was so intense that many supporters of the Brahmo Samaj began searching for similarities between Christianity and Hinduism. This was also the case with Sir Syed Ahmed who had drawn parallels between Islam and Christianity. It was in such an atmosphere that Urdu fiction evolved.

In the first two decades of the 20th century and towards the end of the 19th century, a large chunk of the rural population, forced by famine and epidemics, moved towards the city; these were the early stages of small scale industries in India. In these decades the rural and urban population came into contact with each other at close quarters and, at times, even studied each other. There were distinct changes in the society; the new generation preferred the precise and balanced form of the short story to lengthy and rambling legendary narratives.

In the second decade of the century, Britain acceded to the demands of Self-Rule and an autonomous government in India. In 19 I 9 the Jalianwala Bagh massacre occurred; soon after Mahatma Gandhi arrived on the Congress platform and the Nationalist leader Muhammed Ali Jinnah parted ways with the Congress. These significant events in the history of the subcontinent had their sociological implications.

On one hand, two major cultural groups of the subcontinent had begun distrusting each other; while on the other, the intellectuals and the working classes, the world over, were coming together to fight the forces of Nazism and Fascism. These social and political events provide a background for the study of the literature of that period.

The Progressive: Writers Association came into existence after the International Conference of Progressive Writers held at Paris. Although confronted with communal problems within their country, internationlism came to be regarded as an ideal. It was during the period between the formation of the Progressive Writers Association and the death of Munshi Premchand in 1936 that common factors could be discerned in the works of writers like Sultan Haider Josh, Niaz Fatehpuri, Majnun Gorakhpuri, Akhtar Hussain Raipuri, Ahmad Ali, Rashid Jehan, Ali Abbas Hussaini, Ismat Chughtai, Azam Karelvi and others. These writers could portray a reality which was totally Indian, with all the extremely complex communal, social and economic conditions. The collections of short stories published then, reveal various dimensions of the life of the subcontinent.

Soon after the PWA, the Halqua-e-Arbab-e-Zauq, The Circle of the Men of Good Taste was formed in 1938 at Lahore. At first, this group was interested only in the study of poetry; it changed its stance later. One can understand its approach towards the short story and short story writers from the works of Maulana Salahuddin. He maintains that the study of the characters' minds is more important than the portrayal of their outward lives. He stressed the need for distinguishing literature from propaganda. Unlike the traditional centres of Urdu such as Delhi, Lucknow, Azimabad and Hyderabad, Lahore has always been and still is more amenable to a liberal approach. Although Saadat Hasan Manto displayed an intellectual affinity with the progressive writers camp, whenever he felt it necessary he freed himself from its restrictions. Similarly writers like Ghulam Abbas, Muhammad Hasan Askari, Mumtaz Shirin and Qurratulain Hyder have either boldly or covertly never accepted the real or imagined burden of the progressive point of view. All these writers represent a modern sensibility.

At the time of the partition of the subcontinent, several distinct approaches regarding the short story had emerged. The progressive writers believed that human life could be steered or moulded by literature, others insisted that literature is autonomous. One traditional approach tried to propagate religion through literature; while another set of writers was preoccupied with the portrayal of sex. These trends continued even after Partition. But the riots in 1947 violently shook the world of the Urdu writer.

There was hardly any writer who did not write on the frenzy that was witnessed during the riots. Interestingly, the kind of communal harmony displayed from 1916 to 1920 is similar to the one that is seen in Urdu fiction from 1947 to 1951. The shake-up caused by the riots led to several radical changes. The struggle of the people to rehabilitate themselves created a new outlook, and fresh attitudes became instrumental in promoting a modern sensibility.

The present selection of Urdu stories is unique because it comprises of stories which deal with common issues of life both in India and Pakistan.

The illusion of life cannot be separated from its reality. Till the time myriads of our small sorrows and joys remain and the language to express them exists, we continue to seek a reconciliation of the contradictions of creative expression, even when because of changed circumstances, the nature of reconciliation itself changes. We should not ignore the fact that new centres of Urdu literature have been emerging in both India and Pakistan.

A living language keeps changing its course like a river in spate. The source of the river is the same; the plains, the same; the delta the same and the sea into which it merges is also the same, even though other details of the scenario have been changing. In the river of time, we witness a change in the course of human creativity dependent on the human mind, not on mere latitudes and longitudes or man-made borders.

In the short stories included in this selection, we come across a rich variety of writers at work. Though there are several names whom we have been unable to include owing to limited space, we have tried to rise above the boundaries of ideologies and particular literary centres, so that this anthology may become more representative and unconventional. Creative anguish is closely related to aesthetic joy and in their combination, lies the success of all these stories.

In the fifty years of Independence, the leaders of our societies on both sides have harped upon various issues, but it is the people of both the countries who have been constantly challenging the political rift and it is they who cherish their shared heritage. In Urdu short stories we are not afraid of seeing our likeness in others' eyes. In fact to see ourselves reflected in a stranger's eye fills us with sensitivity and joy. With such experiences of sharing and the realization of similarities, life becomes more meaningful. In this respect the present collection demands special attention. This is by no means a chronological account of fiction written in Urdu during the past fifty years. If it were so, we could not exclude writers like Ismat Chughtai, Manto, Quasimi, Ghulam Abbas, Hajera Masroor, Khadeja Mastoor, Ashfaq Ahmed, Krishan Chander, Bedi, Ram Lal, Quazi Abdus-Sattar and many more.

This collection is actually the shadow of yesterday viewed in a contemporary context and also holds a promise for the future. In addition, it reflects several aspects of the modern sensibility evolved through a history of shared cultures. These short stories have been written after 1960. They represent various patterns of creative articulation of contemporary concerns and a new life worthy of attention.

The responsibility of selecting these stories from India and Pakiatan is shared by both Dr Sukrita Paul Kumar and myself. Ours has been a very simple principle: the presentation of creative moments in which similar attitudes operate and move towards social action. When such similar attitudes emerge from different experiences, they are worthy of sympathetic understanding.

Our point of view may appear to be just one among many other points of view. But then, just as there are a thousand outer aspects of literary creation, there are a thousand within it too, deserving our notice.

We hope our readers will go along with us.

Karachi, December 1997   Muhammad Ali Siddiqui

Translated from the Urdu original by Naghama Zafir

OUR THANKS

When UNESCO asked Katha to suggest a project by which we could show Urdu, the language of peace, as part of a shared heritage between India and Pakistan, we were excited. We decided on putting together a collection of Urdu short stories, from Pakistan and from India, to be published in two volumes – *Bazdeed* in Urdu, and *Mapping Memories*, in the English translation. But I don't think Katha would have even dared to take this on if it had not been for Sukrita Paul Kumar. I also thank her co-editor, Muhammad Ali Siddiqui.

We were indeed fortunate to have the heartwarming support of many. Amongst them, we would like to specially thank –

UNESCO for their sponsorship of this project.

The critics and scholars who suggested short stories and helped us procure them; and especially Professor Sadiq, for his constant support.

The writers and translators for their cooperation.

Sri Joginder Paul and Srimati Krishna Paul, for nursing this project through literally every step of its way. At Lahore and Karachi, Wazir Agha, Umrao Tariq, Farkhanda Lodhi, Zaheda Hina, Anwar Sadeed and others who graciously facilitated Sukrita Paul Kumar's visit.

The Sahitya Akademi for Qurratulain Hyder's story in translation.

Pooja and Roma, for designing this book. And the artists who have kindly allowed us to use their paintings.

Naghma Zafir, Rashmi Govind, Rana, Mumtaz and Lubna, Rustum Singh and Ejaz Hussein. Suman Parashar and R P Singh. The senior editors, Keerti Ramachandra, Indira Chandrasekhar and Shemaz Cama.

And, the great team at Katha – Duttaji, Aruna, Arvinder, Ganeshan, Jose, Manjeet and Vijay; Gagan, Guni, Poonam, Raju, Rajinder, Sanju, Sarnam, Soumya, Suresh – and Swapna, of course ... Thank you!

New Delhi, March 1998   Geeta Dharmarajan

This book has been made possible by sponsorship
from UNESCO, an international organization which promotes
intellectual cooperation to generate a culture of peace.
This book, dedicated to the people of India and Pakistan, is seen
as one more bridge between the two neighbouring countries, built
through Urdu fiction and the many shared memories.

ANWAR QUMAR

THE MAN HANGING AT THE CHAURAHA

TRANSLATED BY RASHMI GOVIND

𝒜nwar Qamar was born in 1941, in Nasik, and brought up in Bombay. He started working soon after completing his matriculation. His career as a short story writer began at the age of thirty. His first story, "Nirvaan," was published from Delhi, in the magazine, *Tahreek* Some of his collections of short stories are *Chandni ke Sipurd* (1978), *Chaupal Mein Suna Hua Kissa* (1984), and *Colour Blind* (1990). Anwar Qamar lives in Mumbai.

"Chaurahe par Tanga Aadmi" was first published in the journal *Nishanat*, October 1995.

$\mathcal{H}$is hands were tied behind his back, his feet at the ankles. There was a noose around his neck and he was hanging at the chauraha. The clothes he wore indicated that he belonged to the middle class. The white terrycot shirt and the slate-coloured terrywool trousers were creaseless. The black shoes were well shined. The elastic on his partially visible nylon socks was still tight, making them fit snugly. It was evident he was very careful about the way he dressed.

His right hand – tied behind his back - held an attache case which hung open. One of its compartments contained a ball-pen and a fountain-pen. The top end of a diary peeped out from another.

With every gust of breeze coming in from the Arabian Sea, the hair on his forehead would blow back. A few leaves of paper would fly out from the open attache case, too, and he would swing from side, to side on the rope. Every time he swung, the black-framed spectacles would slip further down his nose, and with each passing moment, they seemed on the verge of falling off altogether.

The people who had been thrown up by Churchgate Station were standing on his right. Those who had come from Marine Drive were gathered in front of him, and on his left were those who had come from places in between. It was as if some very big leader, a saint, sage, or prophet was about to address them and all these people had come here to listen to his discourse with great devotion.

All these people were familiar with each other's hardships. They all knew why their clothes stung their bodies. Why their shoes pinched them. Why their food was tasteless and their water salty.

Interestingly enough, every man present at the chauraha found in the man swinging by the rope an image of himself. Each one of them felt the noose, the helpless swaying, each time he moved.

The old clock fixed above the portico of the station showed the hour to be ten O'clock.

The NELCO watch which displayed time by seconds, minutes and hours, also indicated the hour often.

The University clock tower struck ten, and the digital wrist watches on the hands of all the people beeped the same hour.

But today's hour of ten was not the same as yesterday's, and perhaps not like tomorrow's either, because all these people should have been in their respective offices by now, behind their respective tables, sitting in their respective chairs. Instead, they were gathered here around the man hanging at the chauraha.

They were all silent – motionless – immobile. Their eyes too wore a stony look, like those of the big black statues around them. And their hearts had forgotten to beat.

"Say something ... say something," they spoke in one voice.

"What can I say? What can I say? There is this noose around my neck. My hands are tied behind my back! And my feet are unable to move! I can't even speak to you in sign language. Nor can I move myself away to some place else."

22

"Where do you want to go? Where do you want to go?" they asked the man who was hanging at the chauraha.

"You tell me – where do you want to go?"

He put the question back to them.

"Where do we want to go?" they started asking each other.

The man who was hanging at the chauraha laughed loudly.

"Ha ... ha ... ha, if not one of you knows where you want to go, why did you ask me this question? You should have asked yourselves first."

"You are great!" they said.

"Because I'm hanging at the chauraha?"

"No, because from where you are, all of us are visible. And we are standing at a spot from where we can see nothing."

"All heights do not necessarily command a view of what lies below. The height should be just right for things below to be visible."

"Are you then hanging from a great height?" they asked.

"Yes."

"Are we visible to you?"

"I can see an ocean of black heads, nothing more."

"Can't you lower yourself a little?"

The man who was hanging at the chauraha laughed loudly again.

"Ha ... ha ... ha, you know that I have a noose around my neck. My hands are tied behind my back. My feet are unable to move. Tell me then, how can I lower myself! On the other hand, if you want you can get me down. You can hang me at a lower height. And if you so desire, you can even hang me at a greater height!"

"We want to bring you down!" the people said.

"I am ready."

"We want to hang you at an appropriate height," said others.

"It is all right by me."

"We want to raise you to a very great height."

"That too is acceptable to me," said the man who was hanging at the chauraha.

"How is it that you are willing to be hung at three different heights?" they asked.

"I will be different from all of you at all three heights. Therefore I will be happy – at a greater height, at a lesser height, or even on the ground."

"How can that be? How will you be different from us on the ground?"

The man who was hanging at the chauraha laughed. "Well, I shall not read the newspaper in the morning ever again. I shall not drink tea ever again. I shall not have my shoes shined ever again. I shall never shave again. I shall never again listen to the radio. I shall never again go to work. I shall not read advertisements while walking on the road ever again. Nor shall I say Thank You! to anyone ever again ... I'm bored of turning the wheel of my life, over and over. I'm fed up, tired. The axis on which that wheel rotates has got fixed in its place. When there is no movement in the axis why should the wheel turn? I am still where I used to be. And if the axis has not changed even now, I will remain there for years. So, now there will be a different axis altogether. New. Unique. Untouched!"

Two men from the crowd climbed the tree on the right. And two others went up the one on the left. In no time at all they untied the knots on the rope and lowered the man to the ground very gently.

The moment his feet touched the ground the man looked at the crowd with the greatest indifference. The strange bond that had grown between him and them just a short while ago, was broken by his cold glance. Despite this they surged towards him with enthusiasm in order to embrace him and ask him what his new axis was going to be like. All of them were bored turning the wheels of their lives around the same static axis, fed up, tired, and they really liked what he had said about openness and freshness and happiness.

First, the man surveyed the scene around him. The papers from his bag were scattered all over the place. He collected them, put them in his bag and shut it. He took out a comb from his pocket, combed his hair, adjusted the spectacles on his nose and wiped his face with a handkerchief. Then, slowly, he started moving in a particular direction. The crowd followed him.

He stopped in front of a tall building. Its gates were locked. "Is it a holiday today?" He began to mutter – "Did I leave home early this morning?" "Has there been a disturbance somewhere today?"

Next morning, as per normal routine, he picked up the newspaper with his first cup of tea, and was astonished to read a news item that said that a man had committed suicide the previous day near Flora Fountain by hanging himself. That thousands of people had gathered to look at the dead body. And that the crowd had remained there till the lifeless body of the man who was hanging at the chauraha was brought down.

BANO QUDSIA

THE SON'S LETTER

TRANSLATED BY TAHIRA KHAN

$\mathcal{B}$ano Qudsia was born on 28 November 1928, at Ferozepur in East Punjab. She and her husband, Ashfaq Ahmed, were publishers of the literary journal *Dastaan-Goi,* printing this at their own press. Currently, she is Executive Member of the Children's Complex. Her important collections of short stories include *Baazgasht, Amar Bel, Aatishe-pa.* She is also the author of novels such as the very popular Raja Gidh, several novellas, and plays for television and the stage, amongst which are, *Aadhi Baat, Ahl-e-Karam, Sitamgar Tere Liye, Buzdil Ek Tere Aane Se.* She has been honoured for her literary and cultural achievements with several awards – the National Award, Tamgha-e-Imtiaz, Graduate Award, Taj Award and others. Bano Qudsia lives in Lahore.

"Bete ka Khath" was first published in December 1991 in *Auraq.*

This is not a tale of Zia-ul-Haq's time–
This did not take place during Benazir's rule –
Nor did it happen in Nawaz Sharif's tenure –
Perhaps it was a little after Saddam Hussein made his entry into Kuwait.

It was summer. Hakim Ali was relaxing on his charpai in the cool clean room with the fan on at full speed. He was reading the newspaper about the American threats and Saddam Hussein's reaction, when the doorbell rang. It must be the postman, Hakim Ali thought, with *Psychology Today or Time or Newsweek*. Adjusting his dhoti, he hurried to the verandah. The postman had left by then, leaving a Kuwaiti air letter on the floor.

Hakim Ali had been eagerly awaiting this letter for quite some time. His only son Muqeem Ali had gone to Kuwait with his family twelve years ago. He wrote regularly, but sometimes his letters were delayed. Hakim Ali opened the letter very carefully with a paper-knife. Before reading it he touched it to his eyes and when he had read it, put it under his pillow. The letter drained him of all his strength.

He wanted to go to the end of the street and get Dr Javed to check his blood pressure. But then, he thought that if he sipped some glucose, he would feel steadier on his feet.

Earlier, whenever he received a letter from Muqeem Ali, Hakim Ali would read the letter over and over again, every little while. And each time, like an eager young lover, he would become impatient to meet his son. The letter was like a tonic, the elixir of life, a magic herb or pep pills that instantly gave Hakim Ali a new vitality, a surge of energy. It made him feel young again.

Before shaving, after bathing, during meals, lying in bed propped up on his elbow, after putting on one shoe, while swallowing his medicine, halfway up the staircase, the shopping bag on his arm, standing at the butcher's shop, a little before the Isha ki Namaz and later at night, just before sleep overcame him, he would take the letter out of his pocket and read it. Several times in the day he would put the letter away very carefully, and then forgetting where he had kept it, he would frantically search for it before reading it once more. A number of days would pass pleasantly in this game of hide and seek. And he would forget for a while that he lived all alone in this small bungalow in Allama Iqbal Town. When he had memorized each and every word of the letter, the anecdotes, the emotions behind the words, the intentions, he would wait for the postman to bring another letter.

But this last letter, it seemed to Hakim Ali, had broken his back! He didn't feel one among the living, nor could he remain alive.

Hakim Ali had been a government officer all his life and always dressed formally in coat and trousers. Even now, during Benazir Bhutto's regime, when everyone had switched to the national dress, he did not change. He had retired during General Zia-ul-Haq's rule and come to settle down in Lahore. Until then he had lived in a government bungalow in Islamabad. Soon after retirement he had to give up his accommodation, his PA, telephone, TA-DA, the innumerable official meetings, formal dinners, filework, intrigues for promotion and his official friends and colleagues.

During the long span of his service, he had made only two valuable investments – his son Muqeem Ali's career and a three-bedroomed house in Allama Iqbal Town. He had educated Muqeem Ali first in Lahore and then sent him abroad for further studies. And for the last twelve years Muqeem had been working as an engineer with an oil company in Kuwait.

When Hakim Ali arrived at this spacious bungalow in Lahore, he had left his friends and colleagues behind in Islamabad. It was four years since his wife had passed away. And with her had gone all the interaction with the family; social contact, customs and traditions. Now he lived alone in this three-bedroomed house. He did his own shopping and himself drove his small car. There were a few indoor plants in the house which he watered himself. The whole day was spent reading the newspaper and flipping through the pages of foreign magazines. Since there was no one with whom to discuss the articles he read or exchange views, Hakim Ali had become a little forgetful. First he found it difficult to remember people's names. Then he started confusing days and dates. And very soon, he began forgetting where he had left his keys, fountain pen and glasses. Much of his time was spent trying to find these things. Saidaan often helped him in this task.

Saidaan took a bus to come to Hakim Ali's bungalow. She was a dark, plump woman with sparkling white teeth. And when she smiled, the smile seemed to reach her ears. Saidaan wore dark orange, brown and yellow clothes. In these clothes, her deep kaththa complexion gleamed like ebony. When Saidaan first came there looking for work, she had two little children with her. The younger one, almost naked, was perched on her hip while a dark-skinned little girl, scratching her thatch of golden hair, clung to her knee. Hakim Ali felt nauseated at the sight of this threesome. He was accustomed to the clean atmosphere of Islamabad.

"How will you work if you bring these kids with you?" he asked.

"Lo ji! Why would I bring them along? They will stay with my mother-in-law, good-for-nothing that she is. Doesn't tire of drawing on the hookah all day, let her look after them and make herself useful!"

"Can you cook?"

"Lo ji – I worked in the Judge Saheb's bungalow for ten years. Had he not gone away to Karachi I wouldn't have had to look for work. Mutton chops, pulao, koftas, I can make everything. I can also cook Chinese food. Sirji, try me out!"

"And what does your husband do?"

"He has been absconding for the last so many years, Sahebji – He ran away with another woman! He had given me talaq, ji."

"Oh!"

"Shameless fellow, was very fond of women, ji ... !" and she started crying. First she dabbed her tears with her dupatta, then she blew her nose loudly and wiped her hand on the gate.

Normally, Hakim Ali would never have employed Saidaan but ever since he had shifted to Lahore, he had an acute servant problem. He also thought that she seemed a needy woman and would not leave the job and run away so easily. Saidaan was generally quite dirty but her work in the kitchen was neat. She was always in a hurry to finish her work by 1 pm and go home.

"Eat your lunch, Sahebji!"

"Wait for half an hour or so, Saidaan."

Leaning impatiently against the door, she would say with urgency in her voice. "My children are small, ji, and my mother-in-law is old. She can't look after the children for long."

"All right, make the chapatis after a little while. I'll eat them."

"I'll make them and keep them in the hot case, hahn Babaji?"

Perhaps it was because of Saidaan, or maybe it was his demeanour and the patient manner in which he dealt with everyone, that all of them, from the postman to the butcher, started calling him Babaji. Sometimes, he was tempted to take a rosary in hand to complete the picture. But then he would feel a little embarrassed. He even contemplated growing a beard, but having been a government officer for such a long time, shaving every day had become a habit.

Baba Hakim Ali faced no problems in this bungalow in Iqbal Town. Letters and drafts from Muqeem Ali came fairly regularly. He did not really need the money, but he deposited it in his account thinking that it made a good saving. Hakim Ali had nothing to worry about. No problems, no anxieties. Except that the days were getting too long. He would finish reading the whole newspaper by 10 am, and even after all the television programmes ended at night, sleep did not come. His engineer son sent him photos of his three children regularly, so he knew who had grown how much. Whenever someone came from Kuwait, his daughter-in-law invariably sent him a janamaz, a tasbih, holy water of Zamzam, and packets of dates.

In the beginning he was delighted with her gifts. Gradually his suitcase became full of these things. Then he started giving them away to friends and relatives in the town. Chacha Saiyid of Uchchra, Phuphi Sughra from Mutthewali and the elder sister of Badami Bagh and other distant relations were not too enthusiastic about the gifts. All his relatives were busy climbing the ladder of material prosperity and they were anxious to give their children a good life. Gifts like these – prayer mat, rosary, packets of dates – made them feel uncultured, outdated, poor. And a little embarrassed.

The last time he had visited his cousin, Bhai Asghar, it was the day of Basant. The sky above the mohalla swayed with multi-coloured kites. Bhai Asghar was on the terrace on the third floor. Scattered around were the children's kites, reels of string, an old tin and other accessories. Items used for celebration of the Basant festival were also spread all over. In the kite-flying match, whenever someone cut the string of a rival flier, a young boy would beat the drum with a short wooden stick. They would all shout with excitement and joy, "Bo kata, there it goes," and one could hear cries from many rooftops, as though goats were being herded. Bhai Asghar was seated on a divan, peeling maltas and eating them. His wife, in a tight-fitting kameez, was popping roasted ground nuts into her dandasa and lipstick-painted mouth.

Bhai Asghar had his entire heaven present on his terrace, he did not need to knock at Khuda's door.

Baba Hakim Ali took out from his bag a crocheted skullcap from China. Then the bottle of Abe Zamzam, dates stuffed with almonds and the Turkish prayer mat, and he placed them near Bhai Asghar. Of all the gifts, his bhabi picked up only the packet of dates. As she ate them she said, "Hai hai, Bhai Hakim Ali, this stupid Muqeem finds only these gifts to send us from Kuwait! Nowadays electric goods are in fashion – he could have sent us a toaster, a food processor or even an electric iron. Everyone has a rosary and a prayer mat. We have three daughters to marry off! Didn't Muqeem think of that!"

The semi-precious stone rosary on the Turkish prayer mat, the white plastic bottle of "Abe Zamzam" lying on its side, the Chinese skullcap flopped on one side, stared at Hakim Ali. When they came down from the terrace in the evening, no one had touched any of these things. Before climbing down the staircase, Hakim Ali turned back and took a quick look at the divan. A crow was pecking at the white bottle mistaking it for a bone!

From that day on, Hakim Ali stopped visiting his distant relatives.

Even otherwise, after his wife's death, he was not able to manage his relatives. Now, whenever his suitcase became full of gifts from Kuwait, he would leave some of the rosaries and prayer mats at the mosque.

At this time, even after his retirement, he still had a bit of the officer in him. He had slowly started going out in a shalwar kameez or dhoti. His friend Qaisar had also retired and come from Islamabad to settle in Lahore. He had a bungalow in Shakarpuryan and a pucca double-storeyed house at Samanabad. A couple of his other friends also used to meet him from time to time. With Qaisar's arrival Hakim Ali felt that now there was a place where he could meet almost all his friends.

One evening, as some long processions thronged the streets, he took the long route to reach Qaisar's house. In his briefcase he had four prayer mats, some glittering rosaries and bottles of Abe-Zamzam. When he got there, he saw a young boy engrossed in washing the small verandah with a hose pipe.

"Beta, inform them inside ..." The boy showed no response. The affectionate tone did not soften him. After some time, Hakim Ali, standing there, briefcase in hand, inquired once again, "Why, bhai, is Qaisar Saheb at home?" The boy turned the jet of water with such force that it splashed on Hakim Ali's shalwar-kameez.

"Hahnji, he is playing bridge. Babaji, shall I tell him your name?" Hakim Ali glanced back briefly at his Volkswageri. He was looking for Babaji in the car! The boy took his time watering the plants and then went in. Hakim Ali was thinking of leaving – he was not used to the humiliation of such a long wait – when the boy came back. The briefcase in his hand reassured him and he went in.

Four ,middle-aged people, who looked like officers, were playing bridge in the room and a little girl lay fast asleep on the sofa.

"Come in, sir, come in ... you thought of us after a very long time ... walaikum, walaikum!" Qaisar said extremely politely, without getting

35

up from his chair, and waved to him to sit down near the sleeping child.

"Just wait a little while, sir ... we are about to finish this hand. Please sit down."

Hakim Ali placed the briefcase on the teapoy near the sofa and sat down by the little girl's feet.

The game was at a crucial stage and all the four players were in deep concentration. Hakim Ali sat silently on the sofa. He glanced around the room – the red wall-clock, the vase with plastic flowers on the television, a cheap print of the Mona Lisa, the tape recorder covered with dust, the VCR lying on the floor, the little girl's loose red ribbons - his eyes took them all in. But there was nothing that aroused his curiosity or interest.

"Well Qaisar, I must leave now ... I will come another time."

"Oh no, no, you cannot go away. Soon it will be time for tea. Colonel Saheb has just ordered some spring chicken from Jail Road. My wife has prepared everything and is waiting ... No sir, you must stay. Today we are celebrating a special occasion. Colonel Saheb's girlfriend is coming from America. She is on flight PK 747! It's a twenty-year-old friendship." Colonel Saheb's beetroot-red face became even more red.

Hakim Ali felt a deathlike silence within him. All four of them were his close friends, but at this moment he found it impossible to relate to anyone of them. He felt like the twelfth man in a cricket team, who could enter the ground with a glass of water, gloves, a helmet or a towel, but was not really a part of the game or the team. For a long time he watched the players, a mute spectator.

Right opposite Qaisar was seated the retired police officer, Tahir Waheed. Hakim Ali had done him several favours officially. He seemed to have totally forgotten about them and looked like a well-fed ram, or a police hawk. The beetroot-red Colonel guffawed so loudly and so long that the artificial flowers on top of the TV turned pale. In spite of his deep-set eyes, grey hair and tight trousers, the Colonel bubbled with life, like a fountain. Akhtar Saheb sat opposite the Colonel. He was a car dealer and his showroom was the biggest in town. Qaisar had managed to sell his Toyota Corolla by displaying it there. But now some people said that his sons had usurped the business and even forbidden him from entering the showroom. That's why he could turn up at Qaisar Saheb's house so early in the morning. Akhtar Saheb's reactions were the slowest. He took his time selecting a card, discarding it and then raising his head. But in the meantime, he would entertain the others with such spicy tales of Christina from America, Gulnarbai of Lahore, Black Beauty of Karachi and Mohasin of Beirut that they would exclaim ... Sii ... Sii ... and lap them up in sheer pleasure!

The bridge rounds went on for a long time. Hakim Ali dozed off two or three times and then he sat up with a start. The little girl had woken up and gone inside. The players, during that period, had talked of land, houses and women to their heart's content. They had no secrets between them. All four of them had reached that stage in their lives when all interesting and pleasurable things are forbidden. Their doctors had told them to avoid fat, sugar and carbohydrates. Women could give them a heart attack, blood pressure, tension and lead to a break-up of the family. Now, because of the doctors' warnings, these carnal pleasures were transferred from the body to the mind and the four of them enjoyed them at the mental level. Tahir Waheed had a full anthology of smutty jokes. Every time he told a joke, showroom-wale Akhtar Saheb's cards would slip out of his hands and then he would spend a long time picking them up from his lap, from under the table and from the floral, carpet on the floor. After they exhausted the topic of women, the Colonel Saheb would start on the subject of jogging and medicines and they would exchange views on what were the essentials, the principles and the conditions for jogging and brisk walks.

These four men lived life supported by their ambitions, envy and enthusiasm. Hakim Ali had given up on these things a long time ago. Somehow he had come to realise that all these were blind alleys with nothing at the end. So Hakim Ali sat with them, like a fly, rubbing his hands. When the Isha ki Azaan was sounded, he opened his briefcase and announced, "Arre Qaisar, I have brought some gifts for you."

"Very good, very good. As soon as this game finishes we will say the Isha ki Namaz on it ... I really needed it badly!" But Qaisar did not so much as look at the prayer mat.

"This Muqeem Ali does not come to Lahore himself and tries to get away by sending prayer mats to us," said the Colonel, and they all laughed loudly.

"He had come last month, for a week. His work is like that. He is an engineer at an oil refinery. Doesn't get long leave."

"The daughter-in-law and the children must have brought a lot of excitement when they came."

"Yes, she had come with Muqeem. In fact I had gone to Kuwait some time ago."

Hakim Ali did not remember clearly exactly when his daughter-in-law Salima had last come! He placed the gifts on the sofa modestly and was about to get up when Qaisar said, for the last time, "Sir, this is the last round and after that there is dinner. Do stay!"

"No, I go to bed early. You must excuse me ... "

"Come, I'll see you off."

"No, no, I'll manage, please carry on ..."

All four raised themselves about an inch or so from their chairs and said good night to him. He had barely reached the door when the little girl came out with a feeding bottle in her hands and lay on the sofa with her feet on the pile of gifts.

From that evening, for no particular reason, Hakim Ali abandoned his friends. And soon thereafter he changed his style of dressing and along with his old clothes, he hung away his old ways of thinking. He started shopping for groceries. He began going to the mosque for the Asr ki Namaz at noon, returning only after the Isha at night. He removed the books on economics and politics from his reading desk and replaced them with religious books. Before going to bed he would listen to some Qawwali on the tape-recorder. He felt that he had wasted his entire life without devotion and dedication to God.

But one thing did not change! In Zia-ul-Haq's regime, he had waited for Muqeem Ali's letters. In Benazir's reign too the letters had brought sweetness to his life. Even when Nawaz Sharif came to power the wait for the letters continued.

But when Saddam Hussein attacked Kuwait, the letter he received left him shattered.

Sometimes Saidaan would come out of the kitchen and, wiping her soiled hands on the door frame, ask, "So Sahebji, has the letter come?"

"No Saidaan, it has been one week!"

"You can make a visit yourself. What is there to stop you? Just buy a ticket and go and see your grandchildren!"

"I don't enjoy travel anymore, Saidaan. I find it difficult to climb the steps to the aeroplane."

The dark Saidaan with her orange kameez and bright shining teeth would laugh and say, "Now it's not possible that you just wish for your children and they come to meet you. You have to go to see them. You have to take some trouble for your children. Look at me ... "

He would keep quiet. He could not tell illiterate Saidaan that no trouble could be taken without sentiments.

He had dispensed with the driver three years ago and was driving the car himself, but with great difficulty. Ever since a cataract began developing in his eyes, bright beams of light bothered him.

When he had the driver, he had another kind of problem. There was nothing much for the man to do, so to pass the time he would laze, sleep and eat by turn. If he had to stay on after 4 pm, he would demand overtime and start to count minutes, then waste time arguing. And then he could never get along with Saidaan. The stout Saidaan's conversations revolved only around herself. The driver wanted her to come out of herself and try to understand his problems. For a long time Hakim Ali thought over which of these two was more indispensable. Finally he dispensed with the driver. After all, he could do the driving but cooking was beyond him.

But driving had its own problems. First it was his eyesight which was getting worse day by day. His reflexes had also slowed down and were not as sharp as before. He did not feel confident while overtaking, especially in the rush hour. But his biggest problem was beggars.

At every crossing, from who knows where, they would appear and hobble up to beg. Some had orange dusters on their shoulders to clean the car. Some would display their maimed and disfigured bodies, and get money by exhibiting their sores, boils, wounds and bruises. Some women pretending to be widows, would hold out their children to arouse pity.

Hakim Ali started dreading these crossings. He was a god-fearing man. But then his approach underwent a change. He resisted the beggars. He did not give them any money and went past them quickly.

When Saddam Hussein attacked Kuwait, Hakim Ali's attitude had already changed. As soon as the car reached the chowk, he would roll up the windows, put on a stern face and stare fixedly at the traffic light ahead. He himself could not understand the real reason behind the changed attitude. Earlier, when he gave money to the beggars, they would invoke blessings on him for a long life, in a very earnest voice.

This used to give him some peace of mind. But now these very prayers destroyed his peace. He would brood over it all the time and wonder what wrong he had done to these beggars that they should curse him thus. He was well aware of life condemned to drag on even after death. But he came out of this hell very rarely these days.

One day, when Saidaan brought his meal laid out in a tray, he was putting on his false teeth after having cleaned them.

"Sahebji, shall I tell you something?" Saidaan said, wiping her hands on her dark purple dress.

"Yes?" He sat down on the low chair feeling a great dislike for eating. He did not know why, but he had been feeling sick at the sight of food in the last few weeks.

"Sahebji, why don't you go to Kuwait and see the children?"

"Why, it is only six months since they came ... "

"Sahebji, to keep alive one must have some preoccupation. You will spend some time in sorting out the arrangements. And then for a few months you'll be happily busy. The children will keep you on your toes. Then the booking of your ticket, packing before your return will keep you occupied. You can't let your life pass by just lying down, tossing and turning in bed. You lie in bed all day like one would lie in one's grave! If you have something to do, some problem to solve, time will pass, shap-a-shap!"

A week later, Hakim Ali was faced with a most unexpected situation. Even in his wildest dreams he had not imagined that Muqeem Ali would send such a letter.

Muqeem Ali and his family frequently came to Pakistan on short visits. He came only twice during President Zia's time. He spent three days with his father during Benazir's rule. When Nawaz Sharif came to power, he came four times. But never stayed more than one night each time.

When Saddam Hussein invaded Kuwait, Muqeem Ali decided to return to his country!

Earlier, whenever Hakim Ali received his son's letter, he would read it over and over again, touch it to his eyes ... the letter would give him a new lease of life. But this letter was an anticlimax, a disaster, it was virtual death for him!

He wanted to read the letter again, but his pulse started racing. He felt like going to Dr Javed to have his blood pressure checked. He put the letter under his pillow and called out to Saidaan.

"Bring some glucose in a glass of water!"

Saidaan took her own time to appear with the glucose and she came grumbling, "Hai, hai, why are you shouting like this?"

"Here, take this letter and read it. But how will you read!"

"Hahn hahn, taunt me ten times for being illiterate!"

"Muqeem Ali is coming back, family and all!" said Hakim Ali.

"So what? I'll go home at night for those few days!"

"Stupid woman! He is coming back for good! Sad dam Hussein has attacked Kuwait. The non-residents are coming back to their land, permanently."

Saidaan only understood one thing – Muqeem Ali was returning home and so she had to go back to hers. The reasons for it she was unable to fathom. For a long time, her sparkling white teeth were locked inside her mouth.

"So what is the big problem? Just tell him clearly that you have performed the Nikah with me! They were not bothered about how lonely an old man could be! How the disease was eating you up."

"The wretched problem should be solved in such a way that it allows me to live, not so that it should kill me!"

Saidaan started giggling, khi ... khi ... khi ... !

She was still young and could roll up her sleeves and give life a tough fight.

Hakim Ali rested his head on the pillow. Under it was the letter for which he had been waiting many long months. But such a letter? Could a son's letter be so devastating, fiercer than the onslaught of several tanks!

ENVER SAJJAD

THE COW

TRANSLATED BY SHOBHANA BHATTACHRJI

*E*nver Sajjad was born on 25 May 1935 in Lahore. After qualifying as a doctor of medicine, he worked for a while at his father's clinic in Lahore. He has written short stories, plays, novels and literary criticism. Some of his well-known writings include the novel, *Khushiyon ka Bagh*, a novella, *Rug-e-Sang*, and three collections of short stories, *Chauraha, Istaarye* and *Aaj*. He has been writing for Pakistan Radio and Television, and has been associated with several literary and cultural organizations. Founder Member of Pakistan Art Enquiry, he was Chairman of the Pakistan Arts Council, and Chief Editor of the periodical *Media*. He has been awarded the President of Pakistan Award and the Pride of Performance Award. Enver Sajjad lives in Lahore.

"Gaay" was first published in the magazine *Funoon*, June 1968.

This story has been translated from a Devanagiri transcription.

$\mathcal{T}$ hey all got together one day and decided that the cow might as well be sent to the slaughterhouse. She was not even worth a dhehla any longer.

Who will buy this handful of bones?

But Baba, I am sure if she is given proper medical treatment ...

Quiet! Trying to be clever, unh?

Nikka stepped aside in silence, and Baba, digging into his beard for wisdom, went back into a huddle with the other elders.

The moment I open my mouth, these men turn butchers. The day I realized what they were like, I also came to understand Chitkabari, the dappled cow. The day these people started thinking of sending her to the slaughterhouse, from that very moment I began to feel orphaned ... What shall I do? They all laugh at me – Why do I take such care of her? Why do I love this bundle of bones so much? Why don't they send her to the hospital instead?

Nikka could not contain himself.

You don't understand.

She is beyond cure. Why throw away money on her treatment.

I am not experienced, yet just yesterday mother added the fifteenth knot to the thread of my life ...

But why not have her treated?

Don't interfere in the affairs of grown-ups.

I wish I could send all you older people to the slaughterhouse.

All of them together caught hold of the cow's chain.

As if she knew exactly what was happening, she did not budge an inch.

They beat her and beat her till she was reduced almost to a pulp.

Nikka stood aside watching in stony-eyed silence. Trying to understand.

Shabaash, my Chitkabari, my gaumata, don't budge.

You don't know what these people are going to do to you, don't move, don't move ... or else, or else ...

The cow remained rooted, turning every now and then to look at him. A little distance away, her calf, tied to a stake with a rope, sat unconcerned. He did not hear the lathis raining down on her bones.

Nikka's ears, too, were getting blocked. Slowly ... slowly.

Once again, the elders huddled together, huffing and panting. It was then decided that even if she did start moving now, it was likely that she would grow adamant on the way, freeze into a pillar. It might be better to put her into a truck and take her there. At least she could be lifted and loaded on to the truck.

Next day, the truck arrived.

Hearing the truck, the cow turned around to look at it. She blinked rapidly and buried her face in the trough where Nikka had just put some fodder, before going off to look at the truck.

Are you people really ...

He could not believe it.

Did you think we were joking? One of them asked.

Baba, give me this cow, I will ...

Another said, You son of a hakim!

Baba, without her, I ...

You besotted son of a Majnu!

A third.

The fourth, the fifth, all the elders – the wretched elders – they are all the same, and Baba who thinks that his beard is a storehouse of wisdom, who knows what has happened to him.

Beta, even after paying the truckwala ten rupees we will make a profit.

You ... you bloody trader, take the money from me.

Here, take it from me. Only, now my fist is full of air, but when ... when I grow up ...

Ha, ha, ha, ha.

When, when I start earning.

Ha, ha, ha, ha.

Then, by then, Chitkabari's bones would have turned to dust. What am I to do?

One of the men had gone towards the trough to get the cow. Nikka followed him. Just to watch. The old man unhooked the chain. The cow, her head buried in the trough and her jaws clamped on some hay, turned and looked at Nikka and lifted a hoof to move.

No, no, no. Nikka screamed.

Keep your mouth shut.

The cow halted.

Heh, heh, heh.

The old man yanked hard at the chain.

No, Chitkabari, no, no.

Will you shut up or shall I pull out your tongue?

Nikka imprisoned his tongue within his mouth. The old man

tugged at the chain again.

Come on memsahib, the truckwala is not your father's servant to stand around all day.

The cow's eyes were bulging.

The tongue merely fluttered in its prison.

But that handful of bones stood rooted.

Nikka smiled. Then was instantly sad again.

She has been sold already and will have to go ... I still believe that if a little money is spent on the right treatment for her, then ... but what shall I do with these elders. If only I were a hakim myself ... This calf ought to feel ashamed, staring on like an idiot while his mother's body turns blue with bruises!

The tongue trembled. That was all.

Then one of the men had a bright idea. He took hold of the cow's tail and twisted it three or four times. The pain in her back made her run some distance. She looked towards Nikka and bellowed loudly. The pain had driven her close to the truck. Nikka's heart hammered.

Shame, you blackfaced man, a thousand curses on you.

The truck driver placed a plank from the truck to the ground and made a ramp for the cow to walk up. She placed a hoof on it.

Don't climb in!

Cut out his tongue. He's luring her away, scaring her.

Nikka shut his mouth once more and moved back.

The cow looked at the plank, then towards Nikka.

You worthless creature, shame on you!

Nikka's head hung down in shame.

What else can I do? What can I do?

She was not frightened yet. Then with suspicious eyes she looked around and snorted loudly, like a snake ready to strike.

My Chitkabari knows, she knows that if she steps on the plank she will be in the truck. But she does not know why she does not want to get in.

They all came together and rained blows on her back with their lathis. The cow's legs shook but she did not move at all. They attacked her a second time and she was about to run away in agony when wisdom exploded in Baba's beard and he struck her hard on the mouth with his lathi. The cow straightened up, facing the plank.

Gasping for breath, Baba said.

Come, beat her.

Nikka was standing some distance away. Detached, dazed.

This isn't going to work. One of them said, after getting his breath back.

So then?

Leaning against the truck, they stood thinking, when – who knows what got into her – the cow turned and, raising dust, ran past Nikka as if he were a complete stranger.

Nikka stood paralyzed.

Look, look, there to the left.

One elder shouted in alarm.

It's but natural. Baba said, running his fingers through his beard.

The cow was licking her calf. Baba's eyes lit up with a crafty smile.

Bring the calf here. We should have thought of this ploy yesterday. We would have saved the money on the truck.

One of them grabbed the calf's rope.

Nikka's tongue quivered. The cow stopped for a moment, thought, took, a step or two, then as she passed close by Nikka following the calf, a curse slipped off Nikka's tongue. The calf climbed the plank and skipped into the truck. The cow went up to the plank, then stopped. Looking at the calf in great bewilderment, she slowly turned her head around to look at Nikka. One of the men immediately lowered a bundle of fodder in front of her. She took a few stalks between her teeth, thought for a while, then let them fall to the ground. She first put one hoof on the plank, then another.

Khuda alone knows what happened to Nikka. In that instant a flood of fresh hot blood surged through his body. His ears turned red and his head throbbed violently. He ran into the house, took down Baba's double-barrelled gun, loaded it, and in a passion ran out. He lifted the gun to his shoulder and took aim.

He looked with wide open eyes. Outside the truck, the calf was nibbling at the stalks dropped by the cow. Inside the truck, the bound cow had stuck her head out and was watching the calf. One of the elders was seated in the truck to accompany the cow, and Baba, nursing the wisdom in his beard with one hand, was shaking hands with the truck driver with the other.

I don't know what happened then. Whom did Nikka aim at – the cow, the calf, the driver? Baba, himself? Or is he still standing there taking aim? Will someone go there and then come to tell me what happened after that? I only know that one day they all got together and decided that ...

FARKHANDA LODHI

REMAINS OF DESIRE

TRANSLATED BY NESHAT QUAISER

*F*akhanda Lodhi was born in Punjab, on 25 November 1937. Till recently, she was Chief Librarian at the Government Library, Lahore. Her published works include two novels, *Hasrat-e-Arz-e-Tamanna* and *Pinjra*, three collections of short stories, *Shehar ke Log*, Aarsi and *Roman ki Maut*, and a collection of essays, *Inshaiye*. She is also the author of two collections of short stories, a novel and a collection of essays in Punjabi.

Her short stories have been translated into several languages, including Sindhi, Punjabi, Hindi, English and Chinese while she herself is the translator of Jack London's novel *The Call of the Wild* into Urdu. She regularly gives talks on Radio Pakistan on Punjabi and Urdu literatures and emergent sociological questions. Farkhanda Lodhi lives in Lahore.

"Vamandgi-e-Shauq" is taken from *Shehar ke log*, 1967.

*G*ori was very young. All those who saw her, her bright eyes, the maida-white complexion, knew she had what it takes to succeed. Bhaji, her father, was not worried about her. It was not difficult finding grooms for beautiful daughters. The only problem was that such beauty had a way of blazing forth, burning many others before turning into smoke.

Gori's mother, Neema, was a simple woman. Born in a dark house in that dark alley, she moved into another dark house in the same alley as a bahu. And it was here that she found old age stalking her.

Bhaji coughed continuously, lying on the floor of the small damp room on the ground floor. Every summer, mornings and evenings, he would sit on the verandah of the house, watching Gori play with her friends on the cemented steps, singing –

> *Thaal maal hospitaal*
> *Meri ma de lambe baal*
> *Payomera sahukar*

Bhaji would laugh, listening to the nonsense songs the children sang, which conjured up images of wealthy merchants crowding the streets, and long-haired mothers, like the daasis of Gokul, making merry. Bhaji knew only too well that the women of this place had hair full of lice, and picking lice from each other's heads was what they did in their leisure. While the sahukars were, in reality, mere hawkers who went around the galis calling out to their customers. At most, somebody would open a shop and come to be known in the mohalla as a seth. But there were only a few such families. The women cooked food on chulhas in the balconies of the chawls, and chatted about all sorts of things. They cracked bawdy jokes, breaking into giggles that sounded like parched rice popping into kheel in the heat of a furnace. The restrained laughter, like lava beneath the surface, inflamed the minds of young unmarried girls.

"Arre, Bhaji's sitting there," some bashful young girl would call out. But who bothered about him! He was just an invalid, hardly a inan.

Bhaji realized that these women were not shallow and ordinary, they too had their own blind and filthy wells. Lost in the darkness and filth, they neither bothered about themselves nor about their surroundings. They were happy in themselves.

Bha's own life had become a pool of stagnant water. He kept feeling that the gali was a sewer into which flowed not only garbage and rubbish, but also a crowd of filthy children. After pondering deeply on it, he came to the conclusion that in that neighbourhood, the women had been assigned only two tasks – to produce children and make rotis. The men too had just two responsibilities – to provide for the rotis and sire children. The younger men had brief spells of falling in love. And two moments of great joy in their lives – marriage and the birth of a son. On these occasions, guests gathered, food was cooked in huge copper vessels, bright shiny dresses screamed and happiness shrieked. Hijras, playing their dafs, would appear at the spot in no time at all, and the youngest of them would clap hands and dance, singing: *There goes the coffin of love.* There would be a shower of currency notes – the galiwalas spent lavishly on such occasions.

Bha had spent all his life in these galis, but he saw them clearly only now, when illness and loneliness provided him free time to think, or perhaps because the doctors had made him aware of it. Whenever a gust of fresh air passed through his small room, he took a deep breath and declared, "What a cool breeze you send, Ai Rabba!"

These people had lived in these galis for years and were used to being there. Such people acquire the skill of seeing in the dark. They are not afraid of dark corners. Darkness does not sting them. They swallow the darkness and become dark within. Then these black cobras would hiss around the bazaars and the galis – "Ai, I shall knife you ...," their favourite knives, tucked at the waist of their silk dhotis, ready to spring into action.

Bha, too, was once a snake in the crevices of this society. There was not a young wrestler at the akhada as robust and smooth-bodied as him. As the saying goes, old age is punishment enough for a prostitute and a wrestler. In both cases, the body is in great demand, an alluring dimension of life that acquaints one with the colours and fragrance of emotions, enhancing one's taste for it.

In recent years, illness had aged Bha before his time.

Above the ground-floor room there was another small room in which lived Bha's younger brother Yunus, his wife and their four children. Peering through the gaps in the iron bars in the ceiling, Yunus's young and frail wife would ask her brother-in-law, "Bhaji, how are you?" She repeated the query every day. Or she would send her child down with something to eat. That is how she discharged her duties as relative, as neighbour. That was the extent of Bhaji's contact with his sister-in-law.

On the second floor, in the room above Yunus's, lived Bha's widowed sister, Begaan. Her two sons had left their boyhood behind and would soon be strapping young men. Begaan kept to herself most of the time, making tassles and tapes for sale.

Whenever she found some free time, she would come and sit at the foot of Bha's bed and whine. She would speak ill of everyone in the house, and gossip about the entire mohalla. "Your illness has completely ruined me," she would tell her brother.

Her behaviour irritated Bhaji. Why should a widow who has two grown-up sons, cry! "The moment a son is born, consider him a young man. But if you are still unhappy, then you should get married again. There is nothing wrong in remarriage. After all Ma too got married again, in spite of all of us being around. Who knows why men become widowers and women lose their husbands when they are still very young. Ma was a widow, you are one, and now, your bhabi, Neema ..."

Bha's voice choked. All of a sudden, acrid fumes from the gali stung their eyes. And, "Begaan!" he called out, happy to change the topic and talk about his immediate distress. "Begaan, tell Ma to get me a charpai. My bones are really aching, Allah kasam."

Bhaji of course lived on the ground floor. And only those who lived on the top floor had the pleasure of sleeping on charpais. The others were spared this luxury. They had no space for a charpai. And also, if bedbugs got into these, where could they be sunned? There were many in the mohalla who had probably never seen the sun rise or set. Yet their pride at being the inhabitants of a big city was considerable.

Bha's wife Neema lived on the third floor with her three children.

And on the topmost floor was Ma – Bha's mother, Gori's grandmother, the oldest woman in the family. Ma lived there with her man. He was not related to anybody, and that was why, behind his back, everybody called him khasam.

And as for Bano, Bha's younger sister, nobody had an inkling where or with whom Bano lived. Not even Bha. She would be found tucking herself into the various corners of these five floors.

The house had actually been allotted to Ma's husband. Everybody in the house, young or old, addressed him as Chacha. In the beginning Bha had not got on with Chacha. But then, he learned to take life as it came.

One link between the floors was the mogha, that gap in each floor which pierced all five ceilings, and on reaching the top, stole light to distribute it to all from there. The other was the spiral staircase. Along these winding steps, each floor was a halting place, a home, and each home was inhabited by people.

Chacha appeared on these stairs twice a day, once when he left for work in the morning and then when he returned in the evening. The tall old man's back was not yet bent. He went up or down the stairs, one hand holding on to his pagdi. His wife's daughters and daughters-in-law covered their heads and whispered to each other, "Ni, khasam has come!" One of the children might call out, "Chacha, salaam."

On entering Bha's small room he would always cover his face with the pallu of his pagdi. Bha always felt like asking, "Chacha, is illness worse than old age?"

Chacha always brought him fruits and other things he needed to assuage Bha's hurt feelings and general sense of disappointment. In spite of that, Bha did not fully trust the man. Chacha had married Bha's mother for his own comfort, not out of concern for her sorrow.

Lying in his room with nothing to do, Bha was more worried about his young sister, Bano, than about his own daughter.

Ma, too, was not unaware of this responsibility.

Khasam: Husband

Bano was not as simple as she appeared. Her glowing complexion and swaying gait were such that as she walked through the gali, always in a burqa, the young men exchanged meaningful glances. But she rarely stepped out of the house. If young men from the neighbourhood went up to the roof under the pretext of flying kites, but actually to try and catch a glimpse of her, she quickly covered her head with her dupatta and ran down the stairs.

Hai, those fair hands tangled in the scarlet dupatta, like leaping yellow flames in a blazing fire!

Sometimes one of the young men would endearingly ask Gori, as she played in the gali, "How is your phuphi?" Gori, her wide-open eyes opening wider, would say, "Unhn!" and screwing up her mouth, run upstairs.

Several proposals of marriage had come for Bano. Why then had the family not got Bano married?

Bha's mother was a suhagan. She must have been a beautiful woman once. She still liked to dress well and wear make-up. Her hands, which the passing years had left wrinkled, were always coloured with mehndi. The dimming lights of her eyes were clouded with smoky kajal and her dandasa-stained lips were like dewy autumn leaves fallen On the ground. She had no children from Chacha, but he indulged her whims.

After he left for work, Ma would come and sit in Bha's room. They would talk about the good times and the bad, about the days gone by and the ones to come. She would give him small sums of money and advise him, "Don't tell that whore."

Bha's mother did not trust her daughter-in-law. She believed that she kept giving away things to her parents' home. She always cautioned her son that there are certain things men should conceal from their women, and some things which women should not reveal till their last breath. If you take the lid off everything then you will fight, she said. A husband and wife should live like two wheels of a train, moving together and yet apart.

Remarks like these made Bha think, What a crafty woman Ma is and what a good man Chacha is proving to be! So what if Neema did help her mother out once in a way, what was wrong with that? Does a woman cease to be a daughter or a sister once she is married? Is marriage such a mortal blow for her, that it severs all old connections?

One day Chacha had not gone to work. After washing out her father's room, Gori was cleaning the verandah outside. There was nothing unusual about this. All the women in the gali washed their verandahs. But a young man who was passing by, seeing her wet delicate feet on the red bricks and the beautiful calves peeping out of her pajamas, stopped.

"Goriye, you are like sugarcane ... I'll die for you."

The young man had barely uttered these words, when Chacha jumped roaring into the gali and rained blows on him as if he would kill him. A crowd gathered. Women rushed to their balconies. The boy ran away.

The most significant consequence of this incident was that Gori was henceforth not allowed to step out of the house like other children.

And Bha held Chacha in still greater esteem.

Chacha's status in the house was like that of the spiral staircase. It wound its way up to the top floor, linking each floor on the way. They were all separate, yet connected. And Ma was like that mogha which admitted rays of light into the dark rooms.

Sitting near the bars covering the gap she kept a close eye on her daughters-in-law and daughters. After Neema, she would turn to Begaan and then to the pregnant Billa. "Ni, Billa, How is your stomach?" she would ask her younger daughter-in-law.

Billo was expecting her fifth child in the fifth year of her marriage, and she writhed with the pain in her abdomen. Billo was a billi, a cat, in name only, in reality she was more like an emaciated mouse, rarely peeping out of her hole.

Several times Bha had admonished Yunus to control the birth of his children. But he would refer to Allah Rasool and end the discussion with the comment, "Who are we, after all, to stop souls from coming into the world?"

When several kittens came from one Billo, who'd bother about her? Billo had only one sympathetic listener in the whole house, and that was Neema, her elder sister-in-law. But since Bha's sister, Begaan, lived on the floor in between, they could not talk to each other often enough.

Ma had deliberately allotted the rooms this way. The young Billo would often tell Neema, "Bhabhi, Ma herself sits on top of our heads with her husband and in the middle she has placed that harlot to keep us apart. I swear, Bhabhi, every night Begaan lifts the cover of the mogha to see what we are doing. I put the lamp out in the evening itself. And to tell you the truth, till today I have not had a proper look at Munna's father's face."

Neema understood Billo's feelings, charred in the fire of jealousy.

She herself had not seen Bha to her heart's content. Earlier there was just no time and now when she had the time, it was not the same. Whenever she looked at Bha sympathetically, he would smile and then start laughing without any reason. And the laughter would be drowned in the cough and the pain. Gasping for breath, he would say, "Neema, after I'm gone you must marry again. You are not educated, you see. How will you live your life?"

Neema always felt like declaring loudly, We, the daughters of the poor, are always lonely. Like the wild fig tree. It bears fruit in abundance but nobody has ever seen its flowers. It is said that only on a particular diwali night do they bloom in plenty. Similarly, there is only one night in the life of a poor man's daughter, her wedding night – like a wave of happiness that comes and recedes – is it a wave of happiness or just a wave on its course which shatters the dream palace of a virgin. And the rest of our lives are spent gathering the pieces and putting them together, little by little.

Neema had heard the legend about the wild fig tree flowering on a diwali night in her childhood, but experience had given it a new meaning for her.

Although Bha lay helpless and frustrated, Fate, it seemed, had given him a long lease of life.

Gori had stepped into her fourteenth year.

She was getting ready for marriage. Strangely, nobody in the house seemed anxious about Bano's marriage. Why was it that neither her sisters-in-law nor Chacha ever brought up the subject?

Yunus was busy making money. He went to the shop early in the morning and returned only after the lamps were lit. That was his routine. Soon after reaching home, he would have his dinner, enquire about the welfare of those who lived below and above him, and then go to sleep.

When Billa came as Yunus's bride, he was just a lad. He was illiterate, but had learnt the art of brokerage from his elder brother. When Chacha started his shop as a second-hand spare parts dealer, Yunus became Chacha's right-hand man. Compared to brokerage, this was comfortable work and more profitable. Street urchins stole car and scooter parts and sold them to him, and he bought stolen clothes by the measure of his lathi instead of a tape. Sometimes a whole week's losses were made up in just one day, and that day he would think of moving out of this Qutab Minar-like house to settle in some open and fashionable locality.

Of the several new trends in society, Yunus had chosen fashion.

A close-fitting, colourful bush-shirt, a foot and a half long, hung on Yunus's short and lean frame. The lower part of his pants were so narrow that they looked like the bottom of a hookah. He looked like a dwarf. All of his relatives were dealers in old clothes. The moment a bundle was untied, Yunus took his pick and then got it altered according to the current fashion. He watched third-rate English films and smoked cigarettes in the manner of secret agents. A pack of good quality cigarettes always peeped out of his pocket, or a case which housed cheap cigarettes. He had learnt a few English words. He thought that it impressed his customers.

Bha did not approve of the airs Yunus adopted. He often told him, "Try to be what you really are."

And Yunus always said, "This is the age of appearances. Who wants to know what lies beneath? Showing off is a great thing, Bhaji."

It was an evening in December. Bha's friend, Meraj, was sitting by his side, in intimate conversation. Sometimes he would stroke Bha's hand and sometimes they would laugh heartily and slap each other's thighs. Suddenly, almost in a whisper, Meraj told him that people were saying all sorts of things about Chacha. That Chacha was, in fact, the khasam of both his mother and his sister, Bano.

Bhaji, who would have throttled a person for saying far less, was strangely quiet, listening to Meraj in silence. And he remained in deep troublesome thought even after Meraj had got up and gone away. It was only much later that the heat of anger blew a new energy into his half-dead body.

After the lamps were put out, he stealthily climbed the stairs, groping his way up. How silent and dark it was! He stopped for breath at every landing, and tried to sense the atmosphere inside the rooms.

A child screamed in Billo's room. His brother's voice rose. "aye chup! aye chup ..."

Bha moved on, up the unaccustomed steps. The light was on in Begaan's room. His sister's whimpering face swam before his eyes. She must be making parandhis, he thought. May Allah grant her virtue, Bha prayed, as he went past.

There was silence in the next room. Neema's room. There were so many memories associated with this room! But the strongest one went back to the time when Neema had come here as a bride. Everyone had made much of her. Then, with the birth of the children, responsibilities increased. And life became dumbstricken.

Bha sat down in front of the room. For a moment, the thought of going upstairs vanished from his mind as if he had started out only to come this far. On one side of the staircase was a chhajja on which the street-light cast a dim glow. Bha stirred the ashes in the chulha. There was not a spark of a living ember in it. But when he saw the utensils lying around it, he felt he had come to life, like he had just emerged from the grave. Fatigue did not permit him to shout. He thought he would call out to Neema, the way he used to when he returned from work.

Memories of those happy days obliterated, for a moment, the new bitterness that filled his mind. The next instant, he was climbing the steps and trying hard to work himself into a rage, remembering Bano. That khasam! I swear I will chew him alive!

Gasping, Bha knocked at Ma's door. When Chacha put his head out, he seized him by the throat.

"I have come to raid you, you old man," he said. "May you die!" Then, in a harsh, hate-filled voice, he shouted, "Where's Bano, Ma? Where is she?"

The question echoed in the entire house. So also all the abuses he had learnt and made up that he hurled at Ma and Chacha.

There was so much noise on the stairs, as if all the doors of a zoo had opened out on to the balcony. Bano stood there, leaning against Neema, staring fixedly at Bha, as if either she or he had gone mad.

Bano had never been upstairs, Neema assured her husband.

Bha reached for the charpai, clinging on to Yunus for support. Drops of sweat stood on Bha's forehead as he gasped, "Go away! All of you, go away."

He then turned to his mother.

"Ma, get Bano married."

"How?" she asked.

"*Somehow.* I need to get Gori married too. After I die, get Neema married also. And I say even Begaan should remarry. Everyone should be safe. Allah Rasool has ordered it, Ma!"

Bha was panting.

Next morning he was sick. It was pneumonia. They tried to admit him in the hospital. But the doctors had no time to bother about ordinary patients. And Bhaji's family did not know anybody influential.

For the next few days, death hovered over Bha's head. Who knows what went on in the minds of his relatives, but he was quick to catch anything bad they said to each other.

What Neema felt, no one could fathom. There was no sign of sorrow on her face, people murmured amongst themselves. According to custom, she should be in a state of distress, no? Wounds inflicted by time heal, but customs survive, like the scars of a wound, and don't people love to wallow in them?

Luckily for all, Bha returned to good health. Once again he started making plans to ensure that everybody was safe and protected. He did not want to die leaving a heavy burden on his younger brother's shoulders, he said. Besides, the family's relationship with Chacha was only a formal one. One couldn't rely too much on man-made laws.

And so once again the question of Bano's marriage, and Gori's, was heatedly discussed. Bha felt he was making proper use of the new lease of life that divine power had granted him.

A proposal of marriage came for Bano. The boy's family arrived to see her. Just one look at her, and they were charmed. It took barely a few weeks for the marriage to be finalized, for the date to be fixed.

Gori's marriage too was finalized around the same time. She had grown up in these very streets and was known to everyone. Not just the boys, even their mothers were in love with her looks. All that her father had to do was to decide to give her to the boy he considered most suitable.

The household was bustling with wedding preparations. Rice was being cleaned, bridal dresses were being stitched, and as they worked, the women broke out into song. Their noses ran and their tears flowed on to their clothes and the rice. They did not have melodious voices.

But the words they sang pierced Bha's heart like arrows. He wept aloud, holding on to his heaving chest. When someone asked him, "What's wrong with you, are you a child?" he replied, "I am a brother, and I am a father. And I used to think I was only a goonda."

His tears plunged the house into greater gloom. But then Bha would take control of himself and say, "Laugh! Sing! Life is very short."

Gori was young and took after her mother in her manner. She did not spend much time with her father. She wandered around the house restlessly, excited at the prospect of being married.

Allah! Such beautiful clothes! Gori's heart throbbed. When would they let her wear them? That's all she wished for.

But Bano seemed to want only one thing - to spend more time with her brother. Bha kept advising her, "Marriage is neither a gamble nor a union of hearts, Bano. It is a game, in which watchfulness and understanding of the situation can guarantee success. The rest is your fate."

Bha had practical experience. And he was determined to see to it that Bano acquired this experience.

Bha had found new energy and started moving around with alacrity, taking interest in household chores. Whether it was because of happiness or the sense of responsibility, no one knew, but the thought of fulfilling a duty had given him a fresh lease of life.

The baraats for both the girls arrived on the same day and both of them were married and sent off at the same time. Like two coffins being carried away.

In spite of the guests, the house seemed deserted. Everybody was sorrowful. How Ma wept, missing the girls! Bha could neither cry nor sleep that night. The pain in his chest increased and frightening thoughts assailed him.

Bano sat in a room in her husband's house, lost and silent, waiting to face the beginning of a new life. Her delicate, mehndi-coloured hands held the edge of the ghunghat. She was alert to the sound of footsteps that went to and fro outside.

Siraj entered the room. Walking gently to her, he bent down to see her face. But Bano buried it deep into her knees. When resistance had crossed the limit, he threw back her dupatta.

He saw Bano's trembling face. Her jhumkas swayed from the reddened lobe of her fair ear. Her black braided hair lay on her silvery neck. Siraj's heart overflowed with love. Silvery laughter dissolved in the golden light of the room. He turned off the lamp.

Siraj was a simple boy. Bano was the first woman in his life, and marriage, to him, was the legal means to acquire a woman's body.

But Bano's first morning in the new house began with her mother-in-law's wail breaking into her deep sleep.

"Hai! We are ruined."

Bano woke up with a start. She was surrounded by screaming women. Bano hurriedly covered herself with the dupatta and ran out of her room. Her mother-in-law was beating her breast and each blow seemed to hammer on Bano's heart.

The walima was held that day, but saying that she was not well, her mother-in-law did not allow Bano to sit with the guests at the marriage feast. Nor were friends of the family and women of the neighbourhood allowed to present the customary gifts to the bride. The guests went away, puzzled.

Bano had lived like an enigma in Ma's home. Here, at her father-in-law's, she was hidden like a vice. She was the disease of this new home. The mere thought of keeping her hidden had transformed her into a disease which did not allow anybody any relief.

Siraj had come to know what was wrong with her and he stayed away from her all day. But at night, he would sleep with her close to his chest. It was her face that he could not bear to see, not her body.

When both the newly married couples returned to the brides' home for the Muklava, Gori's husband strutted about like Raja Indra. Siraj remained silent and aloof. He did not pay much attention to the teasing by his sisters-in-law or the jokes of the women of the mohalla. When the girls stole his shoes, he just lay on the bed and laughed in impatient viciousness. He did not try to get his shoes back nor did the girls tease him too much.

Bha felt pity for Siraj. Of course, Siraj is not like Yusuf, Bha consoled himself. But Bano, who was sitting next to him, frightened him when she started crying.

Bha was the only one who knew the whole story. He had planned his sister's marriage knowing everything, waiting for Gori to come of age. Gori had turned out to be extremely beautiful once she came of age. The dazzle of her beauty had done the job for Bano.

Truly, Bha had done something unimaginable. Instead of Bano, the niece had been shown to the boy's people. The consent for marriage was given by Bano, and it was she who had got married, she who had gone to Siraj's house. Before his departure from this world, Bha had gambled, indulged in an act of deceit which, he knew, would rebound on him. But he was not willing to acknowledge it.

The evening Bano came home in tears, Bha, despite his illness, had gone to see Siraj. Taking the turban from his head he placed it at Siraj's feet.

"Show a little compassion, Siraj," he said, bursting into tears, sobbing bitterly, like a child.

The whole story had come blurting out: A few years ago, when Bha was a strong young man and people were fearful of even his shadow, some of his companions had kidnapped Bano and violated her. They were his friends!

Bha gently took Siraj's face in his hands. "After that I was a changed man. I became disheartened. What was Bano's crime? Actually, we ourselves are nothing, circumstances make us what we are.

"But I agree. It's not your fault either. I have had to cheat. But Bano is a very good girl, Siraj '" Allah kasam she is!"

He kept talking, watching Siraj's eyes all the while with a sinking heart, which, like a miser's, were devoid of all emotions.

And then, as if it was all too much to bear, Bha collapsed.

Somebody took him home. When he regained consciousness, he found himself on his charpai, surrounded by sounds of wailing. The loudest voice was Bano's.

Stretching out his hand to her, Bha said, "I am not dead yet, behn," though he felt as if his decaying corpse had been placed in the middle of the chowk and all around him, crows were sitting on the roofs of the houses screeching ominously, "Talaq! Talaq! Talaq!" He felt the entire biradari, the whole mohalla, was caw-cawing around him. He felt defeated, limp, as he tried to look at each one of them in the eye.

It was Neema who, with utmost solemnity, whispered something into his ear that brought the light of a smile on to his death-like face.

"Well, even the langot of a fleeing thief is good enough'" he muttered. "I am not worried about my daughter, Gori. But Allah, give Bano a son. She will then manage to live her life through," he prayed till he breathed his last breath.

GYAS AHMED GADDI

THE SETTING SUN

TRANSLATED BY KRISHNA PAUL

$\mathcal{G}$yas Ahmed Gaddi was born on 17 February 1928, in Dhanbad, in Jharia district, Bihar. He did not receive any formal education, but for a year he learnt elementary Arabic from Maulvi Fazl-ul-Haq at Gaddi Madrisa, Jharia. There-after, for about two years, he learnt Urdu, English and Arithmetic from Maulvi Qasim. It was in a small library at Jharia, which received well-known literary Urdu magazines such as *Humayun, Alamgir, Khayyam* and *Adabi Duniya,* that he developed an interest in reading. Under the influence of Krishen Chander's writing, Gyas Ahmed Gaddi began his writing career. His published works include *Baba Lok* and *Parinda Pakadnewali Gadi,* two collections of short stories and, Sara Din Dhup, a novella. He has served as the editor of Meeras, a journal of short stories. Gyas Ahmed Gaddi died in 1986 in Jharia, Bihar.

_____

"Doob Jane Wala Suraj" was first published in his book of stories, *Parinda Pakadnewali Gadi.*

$\mathcal{T}$ he rope was taut. He stood on it, poised as if for take-off, his arms tied to a long pole, like an eagle with its wings outstretched ...

He knew they would say, "Walk, walk the tight rope! Show off your skill!"

But how could he? He had never done anything like this before. And why should he – he was being forced to do this. And even if he could, what if he tried and ...

His eyes fell upon the logs of wood being piled up below. They would soon be set on fire. He knew the slightest distraction could upset his balance and send him tumbling down into the blazing flames and then ...

The sun had begun to slant and turn pale. It seemed glued to the edge of a tall building in the west. In a little while, the sun would quietly descend below the horizon and there would be ... darkness.

He had always been afraid of the dark.

Giving him a tight, hard slap on the cheek, his father would say, Be home before sunset. Get the fodder ready and milk the buffaloes. But he was terrified of the dark and the cattleshed was engulfed in shadows even during the day. Night in the shed was darker than the night outside, and worse, there was only one cotton wick dipped in kerosene oil! Frightened and nervous, he would somehow manage to enter the shed, fill the trough with fodder, pat the buffalo and, forcing his trembling legs forward, he would go sit close to its udders with the bucket. And at that instant, into that darkness a white paper kite would fly out of his mind and float out into the sky. Running behind it like a little child, he would try not to lose sight of the kite's string, chased always by the large looming fear that some stronger and older boy would suddenly appear, break the string, throw the charkhi at him and run away with his kite. He would not be able to bear it. If this white kite, which saved him from getting lost even in this pitch-dark shed, was snatched away, how could he stay alive?

And then in the inky dark, a huge rat would brush past his feet. His blood would throb at his temples and his breath would come in gasps. If someone were to shout at him at that moment, he would probably have died.

He was in exactly this state when those five met him a little beyond the crossing, close to the utensil shop. Three strange-looking men and two women. They caught hold of him.

"Abey Fajju, where did you disappear?"

"What Abey, running away from the tight rope?" said the second one, towering over him. "You had gone to piss ... That was three hours ago."

He looked at the first man and then at the other. So scared was he that he could not even protest.

He was not Fajju. His name was not Fajju.

"And these clothes ... Arre Sakhawat, look at our Fajju. Just now when he went to take a leak, his clothes ... "

76

Before he could reply, the second man said, "Where did you run off to? Do you work for free? You are paid a full five rupees. Come on, it's time for the tamasha!"

But he was not Fajju. He mustered all his strength and, placing his hand over his beating heart, he said, "Fajju ... me, I ... Fajju ... "

His feeble voice did *not* seem to reach their ears, yet he kept telling himself that he was not Fajju, but Raffat, with a bloodthirsty father and a tyrant stepmother. He dreads the shadow filled cattleshed more than he does them. Who knows how he had collected all that courage that day to run away from home?

A paper kite severed from its string, he wandered up and down Hazrat Ganj Chowk for a long time. Where could he go? To whom? Zubeda lived too far away – at Masrauli, beyond Sitapur. And he did not have enough money to reach even Sitapur. The mini bus charged three and a half rupees and he had hardly eight annas with him. How could he go to Zubeda? To reach her he had to have three rupees and eight annas. And he would have to buy jaggery worth a rupee or at least a half rupee. Last time Zubeda had said, Raffu, it is ill-mannered to come like this, empty-handed. Is this how you visit your relatives? If nothing else, you could have at least brought gud from Sitapur.

So three rupees and eight annas for the bus, and one rupee for the jaggery, made four and a half rupees. Maybe a rupee or a half extra in his pocket ... how nice that would be! Altogether he would need five and a half rupees!

Raffat was startled. Would he actually be paid five rupees? Mustering up all the strength of his lungs, he boldly asked, "Five rupees?"

"Yes, yes, five rupees, beta, you will get full five rupees," said the big moustached man standing close, resting his hand on Raffat's shoulder. "Maybe another rupee or eight annas if you want, but first, get on to the job, Fajjuay."

Fajjuay? But he is Raffat ... Where is Fajju? But if he is not Fajju how will he get those five rupees?

And the job? What kind of job was it? He can do only one job - prepare fodder for the cattle, milk them and deliver milk to the customers. That's all, nothing more.

He could not even ride a bicycle. Coming out of the dark shed, if he happened to see Vakil Saheb's waist-high child cycling with ease, he would stare, amazed. Such a puny little fellow and riding a cycle! Such big vehicles right in front of him and he was not one bit scared! Smiling and swinging cheerfully, the boy would grip the handlebar and weave between the huge trucks, safe and swift. If he, Raffat, were to handle a cycle, he and the cycle both would be gone ... crushed under a truck.

One day Vakil Saheb's son came right up to him, got down from his cycle and asked with a smile, "Oye Raffat, want to bike?"

"Me? Ride a cycle?" He was startled.

"Abey, say yes."

"But I don't know how to, Shambu Bhaiya."

"Then I shall teach you, in an hour or so."

"No, Shambu Bhaiya, I know how to tend the cattle, nothing else."

"After all, what can I do? I know nothing. What will I do in the show?"

But one of those men stepped forward and put his arm around his neck and coaxed him towards the tamasha. "You will do what you have been doing every day. If you don't, how will you eat? And you won't get your five rupees."

Only if he got five rupees could he board the bus for Masrauli. The bus halts at Sitapur for a while. He would buy jaggery for one rupee at the bus stand. But five rupees is a big sum. He has moved around with buffaloes all day and taking them to the pond, preparing their fodder, milking them, sweeping out their dung, washing the empty buckets. Why talk of five rupees, all this work had not got him even five annas, not in months, not even in years. At Eid each year he got a rupee, that was all.

In the end those strange-looking men managed to drag him right up to the spot in the chowk where the thick rope lay stretched between two bamboo poles. He was to walk on this.

At Durga Puja, wonder-struck and wide-eyed, he used to eagerly watch such roadside shows. He has gasped as the boy walked on the taut rope and as the boy's feet trembled, he has trembled too ... and that blazing fire below! A small slip and down he would come into the flames. The fellow would be roasted in no time. It was not as if the boy was walking with ease. Both his hands were tied to a stick, his eyes blindfolded. Raffat had always felt that the boy walking nervously on the stretched rope was none other than himself!

Every time he walked in the darkness of the cattleshed, he was sure that he was the boy walking on the tightrope with his eyes blindfolded. Who knew why his heart beat so violently when he was inside the shed and why he felt as if he was about to fall into the leaping flames as his foot slipped. He remembered how his blood would gush to his ankles and he would feel stifled. And then one day finally, he told his father he would not go inside the shadow-filled shed anymore.

"What? And the buffaloes?"

"I will not give them their fodder either."

"What do you intend to do then, you bastard?" His father screamed at him so loudly that Raffat had lost whatever courage he had gathered over the months. He was once again empty-handed.

Abbu had risen from his charpai and, inducing softness into his voice, had asked, "But why don't you want to, child? What is the reason? Why won't you go inside the shed?"

"I am frightened."

Sharp came the slap on his cheek. "Saala, and you a gaddi's son."

So? Can't a gaddi's son be scared? he asked himself over and over again, Why shouldn't a gaddi's son feel scared, while others can?

He was reminded of Zubeda and how she had tried so hard to persuade him to run on the long railway track. When he talked about falling she scolded him. "Fear, fear. Raffu, why do you feel so afraid?"

Why? Am I scared because I want to be scared? If someone were to ask Zubeda why she is not afraid and why she laughs all the time, how would you reply?

For a long time Zubeda was silent, her head bowed, her eyes fixed on the floor. And then she burst out laughing. He looked up startled, sure that the paper kite had swooped down to sail past his head.

"What are you looking at, Raffu?"

"The kite ... " the words slipped out of his mouth before he could stop them. He turned suddenly sheepish. It was not the kite that had made him look up. It was Zubeda's laughter!

Zubeda burst into laughter again and she continued laughing for a long, long time. Then, almost as suddenly, she grew silent. Looking sweetly at him, she said conspiratorially, "You want the paper kite, don't you ... that white one, up there in the sky?"

"Yes," he said immediately. "I really love it." He looked up, his gaze fixed on the kite soaring in the open sky. In a moment he was lost, and Zubeda stared at him, wonderstruck.

"You won't get the kite this way," she said, shaking him gently.

"Then?"

"First run with me on the rails and then you'll see." She jumped on to the rail track. "Like this. Climb up and spread out your arms, like an eagle before she takes off. Cut through the air with your arms, like the eagle does with her wings."

Zubeda started running on the rails, faster than he could run even on a flat maidan. She had run quite a distance before she took a turn and, pushing the air with both her arms, came running back to him.

"Like this! Understand?"

Surely one couldn't get the white kite by running like this. Zubeda talked such nonsense. She kept talking. It's a habit of hers.

That day Zubeda had tried very hard to make him run on the rails but he just wouldn't. How could he? He was bound to fall and make a fool of himself.

"Make a fool of yourself in whose presence? Only mine, na!" Zubeda had stared deep into his eyes and said, "Look, tell me, who am I?"

He remained silent for a long time. He could not understand her question.

She asked again, "Tell me, who am I?"

"Zubeda, who else?"

"Yes, yes ... Zubeda. But what am I to you?"

"I don't know," he paused, "Mamu's daughter. My Mamu's daughter."

"That I am, but who am I to you?"

Who is Zubeda to me? It was a difficult question. An uncle's daughter is, after all, a sister, and Zubeda knows this quite well. But Khursheed Appa too is my Mamu's daughter. Why is she not like this? Why does she snub me for every little thing?

But whatever Zubeda might be to him, he just could not walk on the rail line. He would fall. Is it wise to break one's teeth in the process?

Finally he said, "I just cannot do it."

"But why can't you?" The old woman sitting there, her cheeks ballooned with paan, spat out red juice – pchak, "Why? A scorpion stung you today?"

Voice raised, like a scorpion's tail before it stings, the man with the big moustache screamed, "You will have to walk, and so will your

81

father, saale, or ... " and pounced upon him.

"I won't."

"Tell us why not, beta?" The other man came forward and held the moustached man back. "Don't threaten him this way, he will get frightened and if he is frightened, he will slip and fall."

"Yes, he is right, Chacha," the third man advised. "Treat him with affection and kindness and he will surely walk, won't you beta?"

"I ask you to walk with me on the rails with such affection. But you never do." Zubeda turned away, angry. "Allah Kasam, call me a bastard if I talk to you again." She sat there, looking sullen, while he stared, first at the shiny rail track, then at Zubeda and then deep into himself. Finally, she came around and turning to him she murmured very sweetly, "Come with me. You will, won't you?"

He stepped forward and looked into Zubeda's eyes. He saw distant expanses of blue sky in which floated shreds of light, white clouds. The sudden sheen in her eyes overwhelmed him.

He heard himself say, "Yes, I shall do what you say."

The old man with the grey beard and stained black teeth leapt up to embrace him and kissed him with his dirty, salivating lips. "Wah! beta Fajju! That's spoken like a man."

By now the sun was slanted even more, its bloodred rays spreading across the sky. He looked up and found the sun resting on the tall building, staring at him in a mysterious way. What was that pale dying sun, entering his heart through the prism of his eyes, saying? Every day as it sank into the river, what did it say? He tried hard to understand but it made no sense to him. What did it say, every day, before setting?

"Does the sun really convey a message to you before setting?" Zubeda asked, curious.

"Yes, yes, Zubeda, I feel somehow that it does, only I can't figure out what. It carries something in its eyes which reaches my eyes first and then sinks into my heart, as if through a clenched fist ... I really can't make out what it means. As I drive my buffaloes along the river bank, I start to think, and I suddenly find myself bent down, and then ... " he stopped.

"And then what?" Zubeda asked, bewildered and attentive.

"Then darkness descends. And ... "

"And what?"

"And I don't know what takes over. In the veins around my ankles a creepy, crawly worm begins to wriggle and my heart beats wildly." He halted. As if he had no words to express himself further.

"And you just keep quiet?" Zubeda was diving deep, trying to extract a pearl. "If I were you, I would jump up and grab the sun in my hands, and not allow it to set until it told me clearly what it had to say."

"You would grab the sun?"

"What else? And I would not let it set, ever!"

But Raffat saw the sun, which had for so long been stuck on that tall building, finally begin to descend to where the river flowed and the low hills stood. The sky was flushed red – as if somebody had lit a blazing fire below.

The fire was lit! "Yes, it has caught on," said the old man's youthful Son with the golden rings in his ears. Beating the nagada, "Fajju," he called out, "keep standing against the pole a little longer, just a little!"

Soon the sun would fall with a bang, into the lap of the hills and darkness ...

He looked at the roaring fire and then glanced all around him. Hundreds of curious eyes. The noise of the nagada had attracted crowds of people who surrounded him, even people standing at the Hazrat Ganj rickshaw stand stared at him, anxious to cheer him on heartily. The entire area was ablaze with the light of the fire.

But he was not Fajju, so how was he going to perform the act? Soon now those people will tell me to walk on the rope. And how could he? He ... he had never ...

"But Zubeda, how can I convince you that I have never walked on the rails?" he had said in exasperation, looking at her with pleading eyes.

"Like this. Like me."

"You have been doing it all the time, Zubeda. You are ..."

"Listen, I too took the first step one day, didn't I? I thought I would fall. But I didn't think I would die, like you do. So what if I fell? Where's the question of dying?"

Yes, if I fall, I'll only just fall. Why die with fright? And then, he would receive five rupees and with these five rupees he could go to Zubeda.

Now everything was in order, yes everything was all right. He looked at the setting sun.

"All is set, Fajjuay," called out the old man from below, "Tell us beta, is everything all right?"

"Yes it is, yes."

He raised his eyes towards the sky. There, stuck to the tall building, the lifeless sun was peering at him.

Saying what? What was it saying? He looked at the stiff, taut rope in front of him. As soon as he stepped on it, the soles of his bare feet would feel tickled and as his weight rested on the taut rope, it would sag. Mustering up all his confidence he looked at the sun, and at the hundreds of people around, especially those five persons who had mistaken him for Fajju and had forcefully brought him here. He ignored them, as also the blazing fire below and forgot about the creeping worm in his ankles and slowly, happily he stretched his arms. In a low, whispering tone, he said to the setting sun, Just for a little while, only a little while, hold my hand and then I ... And then ...

From somewhere, a boy came running, piercing through the crowds. He wore a soiled, red-striped shirt. He caught hold of the old man's nagada-playing hand.

"Arre, wait boy."

He looked at the old man, startled.

"Why, what's the matter?" he asked, his heart beating loudly, fast.

"Abey, you are not Fajju, are you? You were telling the truth, beta. We made a mistake. Here, come down. Carefully."

Raffat saw that the white kite he was running after through the entire city, had brought him into a horrible jungle. As for the white kite, it was there almost within reach, in his grasp.

"No! I am Fajju!" I am Fajju. I can run on the rope ...

His nerves tensed and all the blood in his body rushed to his eyes. With his lips pressed hard under his teeth, he ran across the stretched rope. He was about to reach the other end when the young man with black teeth grabbed his waist and pulled him down.

"I am telling the truth, the real truth," he whined in a shrill, doleful voice. "I am Fajju. It's me who is Fajju."

"What happened then, Raffu?" Her eyes fixed on the rose-like rising sun of the morning, Zubeda placed her hand gently on Raffat's back, as he lay on the bare floor of the roof. Full of love she asked, "What happened after that, Raffu?"

"I grappled with that saala haramkhor, Fajju, and gave him blow after blow. I said, You son of a swine, how have you become Fajju? What do you know about this kind of walking? But they were too many for me, Zabbi. Those five persons with strange faces, they surrounded me and began beating me so *so* badly ... " his voice was choked, "... and then, Zabbi, darkness spread in my eyes, a dense, complete darkness."

He continued to sob and Zubeda, sitting close to him, caressed his back. In a very strange voice she said, "So what Raffat, there's tomorrow again, and another tomorrow ... "

She spoke in such an odd, sharp voice that Raffat turned and looked up, fixing his eyes on her face for a long time, feeling as if ... as if ...

INTIZAR HUSAIN

THE PALE DOG

TRANSLATED BY NESHAT QUAISER

$\mathcal{I}$ntizar Husain was born on 21 December 1925, in Dibai, Bulandshahar district, Uttar Pradesh. He had received an MA from Meerut College before he migrated to Pakistan in 1947. He started writing short stories in 1948. *Gali-Kooche, Kankari, Aakhri Aadmi, Shaher-e-Afsos* and *Khali Pinjara* are collections of his short stories. His novels include *Chand Gahan* and *Basti*. In addition to critical essays, he has also written a biography of Hakim Ajmal Khan. He started writing columns in English after retiring from the Urdu daily *Mashriq*. Currently, he writes a literary column for *Dawn*. Intizar Husain lives in Lahore.

"Zard Kutta" was first published in the well-known Urdu literary magazine *Savera*, June 1962, Lahore.

$\mathcal{S}$uddenly, something like a fox cub fell out of his mouth. He looked at it, drew it under his foot and began to stamp on it. The more he trampled on the cub, the bigger it grew.

When His Worship had finished his narration, I asked, "Ya Sheikh, tell me, what does the cub stand for? And why does he grow when trampled on? What mystery is concealed in this?"

At this, Sheikh Usman Kabootar said, "That cub is your sensual appetite. The more it is trampled, the stronger it grows."

"Ya Sheikh," I asked meekly. "Do I have your permission to ... ?"
"Permission granted," said the Sheikh, as he flew up and sat on the tamarind tree.

I performed my ablutions and sat down with pen-case and paper. Ai readers, I record this with my left hand, for my right hand has aligned with the enemy and I seek protection against that which it intended to write. The Sheikh too sought protection against hands, for he considered hands, man's allies and helpers, to be enemies.

I sought an explanation for this one day. "Ya Sheikh, an interpretation is requested." And His Worship narrated the incident of Sheikh Abu Saeed – Allah's mercy be upon him - which I record below:

It was the third day of starvation in the house of Sheikh Abu Saeed – the mercy of Allah be upon him. His wife could no longer bear it and she complained. So Sheikh Abu Saeed went out to beg. As he was about to return home with what he had received as alms, he was arrested by men from the kotwali for being a pickpocket. In punishment, one of his hands was chopped off. He brought back the amputated hand and placing it in front of him, he cried: "O hand! You coveted and begged, and so you met your end."

Having heard this story, I said, "Ya Sheikh, do I have your permission?"

His Worship fell silent for a while, and then proclaimed:

"O Abu Qasim Khizari, words are divine and the act of writing is divine worship. Therefore perform ablution, kneel down and sit on your feet, and write it down exactly the way it happened."

His Worship recited this verse from the Holy Quran:

> *Then woe to those who write*
> *The Book with their own hands*
> *Woe to them for what their hands*
> *Do write, and for the gain*
> *They make thereby.*

After reciting the verse, His Worship became sad. I asked: "Ya Sheikh, why did you recite this verse? And what is the cause of your sadness?"

His Worship sighed deeply, and told the story of Ahmad Hajari, which I narrate here, verbatim:

Ahmad Hajari was a venerable poet of his time. Once it so happened that there were too many poets in the city. The sense of discrimination between the perfect and the imperfect disappeared. Every poet considered himself to be a Khaqani and an Anwari and started writing the Qaseeda. Ahmad Hajari saw this, he stopped writing poetry and started selling wine. He bought an ass, loaded it with pots of wine, and went to the market to sell it. People pointed their fingers at him, and said that Ahmad had gone astray. Leaving pure poetry behind, he had taken to trading in wine. But Ahmad paid them no heed and occupied himself in his work. One day it so happened that the ass came to a turning in the road and refused to move. When Ahmad whipped it, the ass turned to look at him and recited a couplet with analogous words:

I stand where two paths meet.

Ahmad says move, my self says, Don't.

When Ahmad Hajari heard this, he ripped open the garment that covered his chest, sighing, May woe befall these times when asses speak verse and Ahmad Hajari's tongue lies locked. He set the ass free and drove it towards the city while he himself fled to the mountains. There, in a frenzied state, he addressed the trees with the verses he composed and engraved these on stones with his nails.

After relating this story the Sheikh kept silent for a long time and sat with his head bowed. I asked: "Ya Sheikh, do trees take cognizance of speech, when indeed they are lifeless?"

His Worship raised his head, looked at me, then stated: "The tongue is not without speech. Speech is not without a listener. A listener is a human being. But if the human being loses his ability to hear, then they who are without this power, acquire it. For speech cannot be without a listener." And so, the Sheikh went on to tell the story of Saiyed Ali Aljazairi. Pay attention.

Saiyed Ali Aljazairi was renowned as a fiery orator of his time. But a day came when all of a sudden he stopped making speeches, and put a lock on his tongue. The unease among the people increased;

they begged him – "In Allah's name please address us." He agreed, "Achcha, place my pulpit in the graveyard."

The people were astonished by this strange command. But they did as they were told. The pulpit was placed in the graveyard. Saiyed Ali Aljazairi went to the graveyard, climbed up on to the pulpit and delivered such a stirring sermon that under its effect, sounds of the Darood invoking blessings on the Prophet began to rise from the graves.

Saiyed Ali Aljazairi faced the gathered people and in a choked voice, cried out: "O city, the mercy of Allah be upon you. Your men and women have turned deaf and your dead are able to hear." Having said this, he wept so much that his beard was drenched with tears. And so he moved out of the basti to go live in the graveyard, where he continued to deliver sermons to the dead.

I requested an explanation to the story: "Ya Sheikh, when do the living lose their capacity to hear and when do the dead get ears?" Sighing deeply, His Worship said:

"These are divine secrets. Servants of God are not permitted to reveal them."

He then flew up to the tamarind tree and sat there.

Be it known that Sheikh Usman Kabootar had the power to take wing like birds. There was a tamarind tree in the house, and it was there, under the shade of that tree, be it winter, summer or the rainy season, that the Sheikh would hold his assembly for the remembrance of Allah. He had an aversion to sitting under any roof. He would say, "It is suffocating enough to be under one roof, where will I get the strength to endure a second one?"

Hearing this, Saiyed Razi's being was so infused with divine love that he demolished his house, donned a sackcloth and sat under the tamarind tree. Saiyed Abu Salam Baghdadi, Sheikh Hamza, Abu Jafar Sheerazi, Habeeb Bin Yahya Tirmizi and this lowly servant of God were the Sheikh's humble disciples. Excepting me, the other five were men of purity and had chosen to free themselves of worldly desires, depend on Allah, and be wandering ascetics.

Sheikh Hamza led the life of a celibate and lived in a roofless house. Under the influence of the Sheikh's teachings, he would say that to live under a roof is artificial. There is but one roof in this world, which is for the One who has no worldly associate. It does not behove the servant of God to have any other roof.

And Abu Salam Baghdadi, he was the son of a high-ranking father. He had severed relations with his father, left home, and come away. He used to say that worldly status was a veil over Allah's essence, attributes and authority. One day, during Zikr, while immersed in God, Abu Jafar Sheerazi tore his clothing to shreds, and set his chatai on fire. He said that the chatai creates a division between the dust that he is and the dust below and that clothing gives preference to earth over earth. From that day onward he was stark naked and made the dust of the ground his dwelling.

Our Sheikh, with the earth for a cushion and a brick as pillow, sitting against the tamarind trunk, had risen above this lowly world. In a divine trance, he would fly off and sit on the wall, or on the tamarind and sometimes he would fly higher up and disappear into the skies.

One day I asked: "Ya Sheikh, how did you gain the power to fly?"

Said he: "Us man abstained from the lure of the world and has risen above the base."

"Ya Sheikh, what is the lure of the world?"

"Your desire."

"What is desire?" I wanted to know.

His Worship told this story:

When Sheikh Abul Abbas Ashqani e.1tered the house one day, he saw a pale dog asleep in his bed. Believing it to be a dog from the mohalla that had strayed in, he wished to drive it away. But it entered the skirt of his garment and vanished.

I asked: "Ya Sheikh, what is a pale dog?"

He replied: "Your desire."

"Ya Sheikh, what is desire?"

"Desire is the lure of the world."

"Ya Sheikh, what is lure of the world?"

"Baseness."

"What is baseness?"

"Absence of knowledge."

"What is absence of knowledge?"

"An excess of learning."

"Ya Sheikh, an explanation is requested!"

His Worship gave the explanation in the form of a parable, that I repeat here:

In the olden days, there was a king famous for his excessive generosity. One day, there appeared in his court a man who was considered to be learned. He presented himself before the king and made an appeal, Learned people too need your patronage. The king granted him a robe of honour and sixty ashrafis and with due respect, gave him leave to depart. This news became known. Another person who regarded himself as a learned man approached the king and got what he desired. Then a third person who saw himself as a repository of knowledge, proceeded towards the court and returned with a robe of honour. There was no end to this. All those who considered themselves to be learned came in droves and returned with gifts.

The king's wazir was a very wise man. One day, seeing this continuous flow of learned men in the court, he sighed loudly. The king looked at him and asked, "What is it that troubles you?" The wazir said with humility, "Jahanpanah, I shall speak if life is granted." "Granted," said the king. The wazir spoke, "Beneficent master, your empire is devoid of learned men."

"This is very strange. Every day you witness learned men coming here and receiving gifts, and you still say so?"

The wise wazir addressed his king: "O master benefactor, there is a parable about asses and learned men. Where all men become asses, there can be no asses, just as when all men claim to be learned, not one can be found who is learned."

I heard the parable through, then asked: "When does this happen? When do all men become learned so that not one learned man can be found?"

The Sheikh said: "When a man of letters conceals his knowledge." "Ya Sheikh! When does this happen?"

"When an ignorant man is taken to be a man of letters and a man of letters to be ignorant."

"And when does this happen?"

His Worship narrated a parable, which is as follows:

Once, a renowned scholar, deeply troubled by his state of poverty, migrated from his city to another city. In that city, there lived a venerable old man. He informed all the great men of the city that on a particular day, at a particular time, a man of learning would arrive in their city, and that they should show him due respect. Then he proceeded on a journey.

The great men of the city reached the harbour at the appointed time. Just as they got there, a ship arrived, in which the man of letters had travelled. A cobbler had also travelled with him in the same ship.

The cobbler was a lazy man and lived on the wages of iniquity. He found the man of letters to be a simple person, and so loaded the scholar with all his belongings. When the two men alighted from the ship, one wore a tunic made of sackcloth and carried a shoemaker's tools. Nobody paid any attention to him, but with reverence and respect, they helped the other man and took him along.

When the old man returned from his journey, he saw a man by the roadside, whose face shone with the light of knowledge and wisdom as he sat mending shoes. Moving ahead, he saw a man without any insight addressing an assembly of high-ranking people and noblemen of the city. The old man trembled from head to foot and cried, "Woe to you, O city! You have turned men of letters into cobblers and cobblers into learned men." Then he bought all the tools needed for shoemaking and sat down on the street, near that man of letters, to make shoes.

I listened to this parable and then asked, "Ya Sheikh, what is the mark of a man of letters?"

He said in answer: "Freedom from allurement."

"Wherein does allurement arise?"

"When knowledge decreases."

"When does knowledge decrease?"

"When a dervish begs and a poet becomes selfish, when an inspired one becomes rational, when a man of letters becomes a trader and the learned one earns profit."

Just then a man passed by, melodiously reciting a couplet:

> *Chuna qahat saale shud andar Damishq*
> *ki yaaran faramosh kardand ishk.*

His Worship called out to him: "O man, recite the couplet once again." The man recited again: When famine took over in Damishq, people forgot love. An air of deep contemplation descended on His Worship, and when he raised his head he narrated the following parable:

In a city there lived a mun'im, a benefactor, known far and wide for his generosity. In the same city lived a dervish, a poet, a man of letters and a wise man. Once, such a bad time befell the dervish that he starved for three days. He appealed to the Mun'im who gave generously of his riches to the dervish. When the wife of the man of letters saw the dervish prosper, she began to taunt her husband, "What is the use of all your learning. That dervish is better off than you. See how the Mun'im has given him so much wealth." So the man of letters went and stood before the Mun'im, and the Mun'im gave him much wealth as well. The wise man, who was heavily in debt, saw the dervish and the man of letters returning from the Mun'im's home with their hands full. He too went there and explained his need. The Mun'im bestowed on him a robe of honour and treated him with great respect. When the poet heard of this, he sorely lamented the lack of regard for words in this world. He went to the Mun'im and recited his poetry and sought a reward. Pleased with his verses, the Mun'im filled his mouth with pearls.

The dervish realized the value of what he had received, and to ensure that he did not have to starve again, he became miserly. The man of letters saved some of the riches, and with the rest, he bought a few camels and some goods and along with some merchants proceeded towards Isfahan – considered to be half the world. He earned profits from this journey. Then he bought more camels and more goods and travelled to Khurasan. The wise man gained experience in the borrowing and returning of loans and started a moneylending business. The poet turned out to be lazy. He simply wrote more couplets, some congratulatory, a few in lament, and received more rewards. And so the dervish, the man of letters, the wise man and the poet became wealthy. But after this, the dervish's dignity, the knowledge of the man of letters, the wise man's learning and the ecstasy in the poet's verses were all gone.

The Sheikh paused a while and then continued: "Sheikh Saadi has rightly said and I, Sheikh Usman Kabootar, also say that in Damishq, love had been forgotten in both ways." For quite some time he kept humming this couplet, and after that he did not speak at all.

Be it known that our Sheikh had a very gentle nature and his heart was full of compassion. He would be intoxicated when poetry was recited to him. When deeply affected, he would weep and rip the front of his robe apart. I write here the last couplet that His Worship listened to and what happened thereafter.

Throughout the night His Worship was restless. Staying awake through the night was a habit with him, but that night, His Worship did not rest even for a moment. When I requested him to rest, he said, "Where is the question of sleep for wayfarers?" Soon he was lost in praising Allah with his rosary and in dissolving himself in His remembrance.

It was still dawn and His Worship had completed the morning chores, when a faqir passed by, reciting a couplet in a voice full of passion:

Aagey kaso ke kya karen dast'e tama'h daraz
woh haath so gaya hai sirhane dhare dhare

His Worship was profoundly moved and said: "O man, recite the couplet once more." The faqir recited it again. His Worship tore apart the bosom of his garment. "O man, recite it again," he said. The faqir recited it again. His Worship was seized with grief.

In a distressed voice he broke into a lament, "Woe to those hands for what they begged. Woe to those hands for what they gained. Then His Worship looked at his own hands and spoke, O my hands, you will testify that Sheikh Usman Kabootar protected you from being disgraced."

The faqir, whom we had never seen or heard before, came in and addressed the Sheikh, "O Usman, the time has now come to die, for your hands have got used to begging."

Hearing this, His Worship wept saying: "I am about to die." Placing his head on a brick, His Worship pulled the sheet over himself and became motionless.

The faqir went away in the direction from where he had come. And I kept sitting there, perplexed. Then I thought I saw something fluttering under the sheet. I lifted a corner of the sheet. Suddenly, from under the shroud, a white pigeon flapped out and in no time, rose up into the sky and disappeared. I lifted the sheet higher and looked at the Sheikh. A miraculous glow illuminated that blessed countenance. It seemed as if he was asleep. I was overcome with profound grief and cried so bitterly that I fainted.

The Sheikh's holy union with Allah had a strange impact on me. I withdrew to my chamber. I was disgusted with the world, and the desire to sit in the company of fellow-creatures vanished. I do not know how long I remained confined to my room. One night the Sheikh - may Allah fill his grave with light – honoured me with his presence in a dream. His Worship looked upward and I saw that the roof of the chamber had opened and the sky could be seen. I interpreted this dream as an instruction and the next day, I came out of the chamber .

I do not know for how long I had remained confined to the chamber. It seemed as if the world had changed. When I passed through the market I witnessed such splendour as I had never seen before. People of all sorts, clean and bright shops, money exchangers, all one next to the other. Trade worth thousands took place in no time at all. The merchants ruled. The Ganga of wealth flowed through. I rubbed my eyes and looked around, Ya Allah! Is this real or am I dreaming? Which city have I come to?

I thought I should meet my pir bhais and find out the true state of affairs. First, I decided to look for the ruined Saiyed Razi. After a long search, I came to a lane and saw a palace there. People said it was Saiyed Razi's palace. I shouted, "In the name of Allah, you men are liars. Saiyed Razi could not have built a house." And I moved on.

Then I decided to search for Abu Salam Baghdadi. A man took me to the seraglio of the Qazi of the city and said, "This is the abode of Abu Salam Baghdadi." I was amazed to see that he had acquired worldly honour.

I moved away to look for Sheikh Hamza, and found myself facing yet another haveli. And I said to myself, I swear to Allah, Sheikh Hamza has acquired a roof for himself. He has moved away from me.

I walked on and asked for Abu Jafar Sheerazi's address. A man took me to a jeweller's shop. There, on a carpet, leaning against a bolster, sat Abu Jafar Sheerazi, clad in silken robes, a beautiful young boy fanning him diligently. I cried out: "O Abu Jafar! Earth has separated itself from earth." Without waiting for an answer, I turned and walked away.

On the way, I saw Saiyed Razi in a silken robe stride past with his retinue of slaves, and I lost my patience. I moved forward, lifted the heavy skirt of his robe and said, "O you, who was left behind to uphold the memory of a venerable family, O Saiyed-us-Sadaat, have you given up the sackcloth to cover yourself with silk?" He was abashed, and I turned towards my chamber, weeping. I continued to weep for a long time, saying, I swear to Allah I am left all alone.

The next day, I presented myself at the Sheikh's mazar-e-sharif. There I found Habeeb Bin Yahya Tirmizi seated on a mat, wrapped in a blanket. I sat by his side and said, "O Habeeb, have you noticed how the world has changed, how our companions have forgotten the teachings of our Sheikh and turned away from the path?" Regret was writ large on his face. Sighing deeply, he said: "There is no doubt that the world has changed. Our companions have forgotten the teachings of the Sheikh and they have given up their chosen path."

I said, "Death to the slave of the dinar, and death to the slave of the dirham!"

The same evening, a messenger from Abu Salam Baghdadi came to me. "Come," he said, "your old friend wants to see you." When I reached there, I found Habeeb Bin Yahya Tirmizi also present. Furrowing his brow, Abu Salam Baghdadi said, "You, Abul Qasim Khizari, you accused us of deviating from the teachings of the Sheikh and you shouted death to us." I looked angrily at Habeeb Bin Yahya Tirmizi and then looked straight into the eyes of Abu Salam Baghdadi and said, "Abu Salam, will you prevent me from saying what the Prophet had said and which the Sheikh had made a habit of repeating?" I then recited the Hadith in full.

"Death to the slave of the dinar, death to the slave of the dirham, and death to the slave of the black blanket, and to the one who dons tom clothes."

Meanwhile, a dastarkhwan was spread out on the floor and on it were arranged dishes of food of different varieties and colours. Abu Salam Baghdadi invited me, "O friend, partake of the food." But I was content to drink cold water. I said: "O Abu Salam Baghdadi, it is daylight and we are to fast during this time." Hearing this, Abu Salam Baghdadi said, "You speak the truth, Abul Qasim." And he began to eat. Habeeb Bin Yahya Tirmizi too wept on hearing this, and then he too ate to his heart's content.

When the dastarkhwan was folded, a dancer came in with a retinue of slave girls. I saw her and stood up. Abu Salam Baghdadi said in an insistent voice, "O friend, be seated." I repeated, "O Abu Salam Baghdadi, it is daylight and we are to fast during this time." And I left the place. The tapping of the harlot's feet and the jingling of her ghungroos followed me. I stuffed my fingers into my ears and walked on.

When I entered my chamber, something clammy struggled up into my throat and wriggled out of my mouth. I lit the lamp and searched every nook and corner of the chamber, but could not see anything. I told myself, Perhaps it was only my imagination. And I lay on the mat and went to sleep.

When I woke up the next day, I went up to Habeeb Bin Yahya Tirmizi, and saw that a pale dog lay asleep on his mat. I said: "O son of Yahya Tirmizi, you have surrendered yourself to desire, and become a hypocrite." He wept and said, "I swear by Allah, I am one of your associates and I go to your companions to remind them of the Sheikh's path."

Then I saw the faithful at the grave of the Sheikh - may it be filled with light by Allah's grace – offering gold and silver, and I said: "O son of Yahya, woe to you, you have converted the Sheikh, after his death, into a man desirous of wealth. What do you do with all this gold and silver?" Habeeb Bin Yahya Tirmizi wept again and said,

"I swear by Allah, this gold and silver is equally divided between Saiyed Razi, Abu Jafar Sheerazi, Abu Salam Baghdadi and me. I distribute my share among those who do not have sufficient money to meet their needs. I am aware that I am fated to remain with this mat."

I moved on, and when I passed by Saiyed Razi's palace, I saw a large pale dog standing at its gate. And I found the same pale dog in front of Sheikh Hamza's haveli, and I found it asleep on Abu Jafar Sheerazi's large cushion. It was standing with its tail raised in the seraglio of Abu Salam Baghdadi. And I asked myself, a Abul Qasim, why have you come here? And Abul Qasim said, to persuade Abu Salam Baghdadi to take the Sheikh's path.

That night I found Habeeb Bin Yahya Tirmizi seated at Abu Salam Baghdadi's dastarkhwan. Abu Salam Baghdadi said to me, "O friend, partake of this food." I contented myself with cold water, and said, "O Abu Salam Baghdadi, it is daylight and we are to fast during this time." Salam Baghdadi wept, and said, "O friend, that is true." And when the dancer appeared, I withdrew from there. And the tapping of feet and the jingling of ghungroos followed me for some distance. But I put my fingers into my ears and moved on.

On the third day, I once again went around the city and found no change in what I had witnessed the last two days. In the night I found myself standing again at Abu Salam Baghdadi's door. I knew that I had gone there to remind Abu Salam Baghdadi of the teachings of the Sheikh. So, I did not ask myself any questions and walked in. Habeeb Bin Yahya Tirmizi was there as usual to have his fill. Abu Salam Baghdadi said to me, "O friend, partake of food." This was my third day of starvation, and on the dastarkhwan, among other dishes, was zafrani pulao, once a great favourite of mine. I ate one mouthful and withdrew my hand. Then I drank cold water, and said: "It is daylight, and we are to fast during this time."

This time, Abu Salam Baghdadi, instead of weeping, heaved a sigh of relief and said: "O friend, you speak the truth." The dancer entered then, and I glanced at her. At her face, splendidly red, eyes like cups of wine, firm breasts and stout thighs, belly like a small sandalwood plank, and a roundish bowl-like navel. She wore such a transparent garment that the sandalwood plank, the round bowl and the hips, the silvery calves, everything was prominently visible. I felt as if I had taken another mouthful of the aromatic zafrani pulao. A sensual tremor ran through my fingertips and my hands started going out of control.

I remembered the Sheikh's words about hands. I jumped up, alarmed that Abu Salam Baghdadi had not insisted that I partake of the food that day. And the tapping of feet and the jingling of ghungroos of the whore followed me for quite a distance, exercising a sweet effect on me.

When I reached home and entered the chamber, what did I see! On my mat lay a pale dog, asleep. I froze like an engraving in stone, and broke out in a cold sweat. I began to beat the dog, but it slipped into my robe and disappeared. I was besieged by anxiety. Sleep vanished from my eyes and tranquillity departed from my heart. I cried for help. "O Allah, have mercy upon me, my heart is afflicted with filth and the pale dog has found a place inside me." I pleaded for help, I prayed. But my heart remained restless.

I was then, all at once, reminded of Abu Ali Rudbari who had for some time been afflicted with the disease of temptation. Early one morning before daybreak, he went to the river and remained there till the sun rose. His heart filled with grief during this time and he pleaded with god: "Ai Bar-e-Khudaya, give me peace." An invisible voice from the river spoke, "Is there peace in knowledge?" And I said to myself, a Abul Qasim Khizari, leave this place, for here, outside of you and inside you, pale dogs have come into existence, and have deprived you of your tranquillity.

I gave my chamber one last look, left behind the rare books on logic and jurisprudence which I had so carefully collected over the years, tucked under my arm just the book of sayings of the Sheikh, and moved out of the city.

As I left the city the ground seemed to grab my feet and prevent me from leaving. I was strongly reminded of the Sheikh's aromatic assemblies. That land, which I had regarded as pure and sacred, was pleading with me not to leave it. Those streets, which had the honour of having kissed the feet of the Sheikh, called out to me. Hearing them, I wept and lamented: "Ya Sheikh, your city is concealed under the roofs and has distanced itself from the sky. And your foot-dragging companions have revolted against you. They have made their own roof against that which has no equal. They have grown crops from that soil, and the pale dog has acquired respectability and the most excellent of Allah's creations is disgraced, and there is no place for me here, so I leave your city." I hardened my heart and moved on.

I walked far, so far that my feet were blistered and I was panting. Then, unexpectedly, something struggled out of my throat and fell at my feet. I looked down and was astonished to see a fox cub rolling at my feet. I decided to crush it, trampling it under my feet. But the fox cub swelled to corpulence. I continued to trample it and it grew larger, it kept growing till it turned into a pale dog. With all my strength, I kicked the pale dog and trampled it thoroughly under my feet and moved forward. And I said, "I swear by Allah, I have crushed my pale dog," and, kept walking till the blisters on my feet became boils, and my toes split, and the soles were covered with blood.

But then the pale dog, which I had trampled and left behind, reappeared – I don't know from where – and stood blocking my way.

I fought with it and tried hard to remove it from my path. But it did not budge a hair's breadth. I was tired, fatigued – I had become small and that pale dog had swelled and become monstrous. I cried out for assistance, in the court of Rabb-ul-Izzat: "Ai sustainer of life! Mankind has become small and the pale dog has grown large! I wanted to trample it under my feet, but it vanished into the skirt of my garment." I looked at my cracked toes and blood-soaked soles, and at the blisters that had turned into boils, and wept at my condition. If only I had not migrated from the city of the Sheikh!

My attention was then diverted towards something else. I remembered the aromatic zafrani pulao, and she who possessed the sandalwood plank and round cups. And I let my thoughts run to the grave of the Sheikh being showered with gold and silver. I thought, Doubtless, the Sheikh's disciples have deviated from his teachings, and Habeeb Bin Yahya Tirmizi has chosen the path of opposition. I thought, Doubtless, the book of sayings of the Sheikh is in my possession, and it is only proper that I go back to the city, revise it, make it acceptable to the people, and make arrangements for its dissemination. Also, I should write the biography of the Sheikh in such a manner that it is liked by our companions and is not offensive to anybody.

But I was suddenly reminded of the Sheikh's words, Hands are the enemies of mankind, and I thought my hands would harm me. The same night, when I was thinking of going to sleep, I saw that the pale dog had appeared again and was asleep on my mat. I beat it and tried to push it away from my mat. I battled with it. All night, the pale dog and I grappled with each other. Sometimes it was trampled under my feet, and it would become small and I would grow large. Sometimes it rose above me and I became small while it grew large. Soon it was morning. The pale dog's strength decreased and it slipped into the skirt of my garment and vanished.

Ever since then, a fight has been on between me and the pale dog. The details of this fierce struggle to overcome desire are too many and its subtleties too numerous - I shall overlook these here lest this journal become too long. Sometimes, it is the pale dog that overpowers me and sometime it is I who gain over it. Sometimes I grow large and it is reduced to a fox cub. Sometimes, it keeps growing and I am diminished, and the thought of the aromatic zafrani pulao, of the sandalwood plank, and of the round cups, oppresses me.

The pale dog says, When all have become pale dogs, then it is much worse to remain human. And I cry for assistance: "Ai Rabbbul-Izzat, for how long should I wander, in the shadow of the trees, away from mankind? For how long should I live on half-ripe fruits and lie on rough sackcloth?" Then my feet make a move towards the city.

But I am reminded of the Sheikh's command: Returning footsteps are the enemy of those who take to the path of Muhammad to reach Allah. And I would punish my feet again and walk such a long distance, with my back towards the city, that their sales would be covered with blood. And I would punish my hands by making them pick up the stones and pebbles on the road. Ai Rabb-ul-Izzat, I have given so much punishment to my enemies that the soles of my feet are covered with blood, from picking stones my fingertips have turned into sores, my skin is darkened in the heat of the sun, and my bones have started melting. My sleep has burnt out, and I am robbed of my days. The world has become unbearable for me. I am one who keeps fasts, and day by day the fasts are growing longer.

From that day onward, I became lean. But the pale dog comes every night and lies on my mat. I have no respite, my mat is possessed by another. The pale dog is exalted and mankind despised. Once again I remember Abu Ali Rudbari – the consent of Allah be upon him – and I kneel by the riverside, my feet tucked under me. My heart is seized with grief. And I lament, "Bar-e-Illaha, give me peace, peace, peace."

I lamented all night and kept looking towards the river. And all night, strong dusty winds passed through the ashamed trees. And all night, the leaves kept falling from the trees. I took my eyes off the river, and viewed my dusty body, and viewed the heaps of pale leaves around me. And I said, "These are my desires and wishes. I swear by Allah, I am now free from desire, and I have become like a naked tree in autumn." But it was dawn when I felt a sweet juice pouring into the tip of my fingers, as if they had touched that sandalwood plank, and felt the round golden cups and the soft silvery calves, as if the hands were playing with gold and silver, and with it came the jingling of dirham and dinar.

I open my eyes, and in that dim light, I see a frightful spectacle. The pale dog stands with its tail erect, its hind legs inside the city and its forelegs on my mat, and its wet, warm nose touching the fingers of my right hand. I look at my right hand as if it is the severed hand of Abu Saeed – may Allah's mercy be upon him – as it lies apart from me. And addressing it, I say, "O my hand, O my companion, you have aligned with the enemy." And I close my eyes and pray: "Bar-e-Illaha, give me peace, peace, peace."

JEELANI BANO

JOY

TRANSLATED BY NAGHMA ZAFIR

$\mathcal{J}$eelani Bano was born on July 16, 1936, in Badayun in Uttar Pradesh. She started writing stories in 1955, and since then, nine short story collections of hers, as also two novels and two novellas, have been published. Some of her well-known short stories are:

"Mein," "Mom ki Mariam," "Nirvan," "Roshni ke Deewar," "Paraya Ghar," "Joy." Her stories have also been translated into other Indian and foreign languages while her novels, *Aiwan-e-Ghazal* and *Barish-e-Sang*, are available in both Hindi and English translations. She has received the Ghalib Award (1978), the Doshiza Award (1983), the Sovietland-Nehru Award (1985) and the Nuqoosh Award, Lahore (1991). Jeelani Bano also writes for television, especially for women-based programmes. She has been involved in development programmes in the rural areas of Andhra Pradesh, and is committed to the cause of equality for rural women. Jeelani Bano lives in Hyderabad, India.

"Joy" was first published in her collection, *Such-ke-Siwa*, 1997.

$\mathcal{J}$oy attracts the scattered fragments of this household like a magnet. "Bow-wow-wow." It's his bark that assures everyone in this house – my house – where each one has a grouse against the other, that it is morning. Nothing delights my family more than hurting each other, thus avenging themselves for all the disappointments and failures that the world outside has heaped upon them.

But Joy doesn't let them do so. These days, the entire household runs according to his wishes. If someone wants to shower affection, it is Joy who is the recipient; if someone laughs, it is at Joy's antics. We are all well acquainted with his moods, his likes and dislikes. Sometimes I feel as if it is Joy, not I, who is the head of this family. Indeed it is Joy who supervises each and every household chore. When people are leaving the house, it is he who sees them off at the gate. Those who want to come in are looked upon with suspicion and are allowed in only when Joy is satisfied with their credentials. He keeps watch over the kitchen too – the cats peeping over the wall, the crows creating a din in the groves, the stranger at the door ringing the bell. All these responsibilities leave him exhausted.

"Bow-wow-wow ... Wake up!" He shakes me out of my sleep just before daybreak. "You aren't destined to have pleasant dreams, so let's go chase a beautiful thought down the street ... some beautiful, interesting adventure ... "

"Unhh ... " I turn my face away wiping off the imprint of his moist affection.

"Kun ... kun ... kun ... " Joy jumps on to my bed with a whimper. My wife Rama takes sleeping pills, so Joy knows that he won't be kicked for his disobedience.

"How the hell do you manage to open the door and get in?" I hold him by the scruff of his neck and shove him down. Rama and I observe changing seasons – when I feel hot, she begins to feel cold. Before we go off to sleep, we exchange complaints, followed by a volley of accusations and counter-accusations ... To avoid such a situation both of us have spread a network of live wires around us ... Now, if I want to get close to Rama I have to turn off and turn on several switches. But Joy is not bothered. He jumps across all these to shower his love on me. How can one help but kiss him in return?

Rama expresses distaste ... "Chhi -chhi-thoo-thoo!" But soon after, as she sits yawning in bed, Joy climbs into her lap and extorts his due share of affection. When I catch her in the act, she bows her head in embarrassment as if I've caught her red-handed with a lover.

I am an unsuccessful businessman. Any loss in business increases my blood pressure, but when I see the rising price index on the morning television I begin to feel reassured once again – I want to close my eyes and dream of becoming a millionaire.

The doctor has asked me to go for morning walks. Others in the house may forget this but Joy never does. Once we are out on the road, like an obedient child Joy trots beside me, watchful of my moods, but soon enough some wayside scene allures him and he is compelled to run towards it. I hold Joy by his leash but it seems as if it is Joy who has put a chain around my neck. He leads me in whichever direction he pleases.

After having climbed down four storeys, I want to just sit on the bench in the lawn, but for Joy the early morning light holds uncountable hopes and promises. The bitches that passed this way the night before have left their scents behind them. Joy's nostrils flare, he breathes deeply, and suddenly takes off, as if he knows exactly where he is going.

Joy too is an artist, a dreamer – and he wants to run ahead in pursuit of his new creation. And I, caught in the choking noose of complicated business concerns and wanting to break free, to sit in the fresh open air and write a poem or simply chase a new thought, I run behind him panting – I, the unsuccessful businessman, the mediocre poet, one who all his life has merely dreamed of getting into the big league some day.

"Daddy, did you ever consult anyone before going into business?" "Daddy, your classmate is such a well-known doctor. Why didn't you take up medicine?"

I become anxious when my children put these questions to me.

"Arre, he has always failed in whatever he tried his hand at!" Rama would heave a sigh and slap her forehead, shaking her head.

I would find a strange haze engulfing me from all sides.

Rama is as bitter as she was beautiful. I had lost my heart to this winsome girl who had oozed charm, like a gulab jamun dripping with syrup. But from the day we tied the knot and climbed the stairway of my house, side by side, it has seemed to me that I climb a mountain While she stands by, laughing. Rama had put a noose around my neck. I too have a noose around Joy's neck, yet I am running with him.

Both of us are panting. I know very well that this pursuit is futile, that there is nothing to be found on the road that Joy has taken, but the very search and the hope of chancing upon some unexpected happiness drives him crazy. He looks intently at the crowd of people passing by, the cars and the scooters, and starts barking at those whom he doesn't fancy.

"You fool! That was a minister's car. Did you have to bark at it?" Hearing this, Joy lifts his leg at the nearest lamp-post and pretends to pee. He has done this earlier too, to express disapproval.

The faint suspicion of light on the horizon has changed to convincing daylight. She's not turned up yet.

The two of us stare into the distance. She has definitely crossed this path the night before. Joy once again flares his nostrils and picks up her scent. Suddenly Rosy's distant bark distracts him. Raising his head to the residents of Ashiana he sends out his order – "Bow-wow-wow – set Rosy free – don't shut her up behind bars – come down, dear Rosy ... "

"You really are an idiot!" I am angry. She has been locked up. Her fat mistress hates going for walks. She keeps her dainty virgin bitch behind barred windows, away from amorous dogs so that they, like Joy, can bark themselves crazy.

"Don't create such a din, yaar."

"For all you know, if you actually get her you may regret it even more."

Joy continues to hunt for the clues of his many loves at various places. He pauses at a spot and begins to dig with vigour; then, overcome with desire, he leaps up and down. I get weary - the road that lies ahead of this one holds no interest for me. My job is merely to hold on to Joy's leash and to walk behind him.

The doctor has asked me to walk about five kilometres each day.

I have measured this distance several times in my head – a bit ahead of the petrol pump, close to the ice-cream parlour – but Joy doesn't acknowledge any limits.

While he whines for Rosy the floating feather of a bird becomes the harbinger of new pleasures for him. Careering and growling he pounces at it, grabs it in his mouth, puts it in my lap.

The world holds so many pleasures and delights for Joy, while I sit empty-handed on the footpath. A woman's angry glance goads him to run ahead once again – the leash does not bother him any more. All the beautiful women walking on the road give Joy a smile, children whistle at him, this bright sunshine is for him, the cool breeze blows for him – fragrant smells, unusual scenes, all these are Joy's interesting toys. I have only this harsh daylight to accompany me, a day filled with complicated business matters, a sun that grows hotter by the minute.

All those who are out for their morning walk greet Joy. Patting a dog is taken to be a sign of being cultured, but to talk to someone as useless as I am, is not acceptable in highbrow society. That is why when Joy is with me he always has a separate identity; and when I am alone I am always ignored. I am a mere human being.

We were walking towards home with our heads bent when we suddenly saw Pinky along with her mother down the road, and our hearts perked up.

"Joy … ju … ju," she whistles at Joy when she meets us on the road. The moment Joy hears her voice he runs towards her, entwines himself around her fair calves, tugs at her frock, pushes her, and careen; around her.

Pinky likes both of us. She had once heard me recite my poems on a television show and had asked me for my autograph. Pinky's Soothing smile, the warmth of her proximity and her approving glance relax me. She comes to our house sometimes to play with Joy. Although Rama has had a nasty quarrel with her mother about spoiling the lawns, Pinky is considered to be Archana's friend, and now she is Joy's friend too. In any case, all the neighbourhood kids refer to our house as Joy's house.

The minute Pinky enters the house, Joy bounds towards her from under my chair. He begins to jostle her, whimpering with pleasure. Pinky always carries with her a bar of chocolate or a small ball, for him. The entire house resounds with the racket they create. Running behind Joy, Pinky sometimes comes into my room and I jump up in confusion. Inevitably, I misplace something or the other, turn the entire room upside down. Joy would pick up the paper from my table and put it in the dustbin. Everyone would begin to laugh.

"He has really become such a nuisance." Archana joins them in their game. "Whenever he dislikes something he throws it in the dustbin."

"Really?"

"Yes, all our missing things are found in the dustbin these days, only yesterday Mummy's lipstick ... "

"Archana, stop making such a noise – I have a headache." Rama's scolding puts a stop to their laughter.

"Bow-wow-wow – shut up, you nag!" Joy chides Rama. Though enraged, Rama pretends to forgive Joy just because he is an animal.

Whenever things like this happen, it would be some time before I stop laughing – as if Joy had fulfilled a long-held desire of mine. That somebody could actually scold Rama ... just imagine!

The newspaper lies on the breakfast table. A fierce battle rages in the world. Around the breakfast table too, there is an intense struggle for power amongst the influential forces of this household. Romi has decided to leave for America after getting his share of the family property. He probably wants to rid himself of a stupid father and a stubborn mother. Archana has decided to give up her studies and get married to a twice-divorced stage actor. Rama finds it impossible to accept that her orders could be disobeyed in this household, and she holds me responsible for the entire mess. Surely, only an impoverished and cowardly father could be so effective!

Kuwait is a small nation. Overnight it has been seized by a world super power. This bit of news mingles with the slices of bread and marmalade and leaves a bitter taste in the mouth.

On my way back home I practise the dialogues I am going to exchange with Rama and the children. Romi is the first to notice us in the doorway, he whistles at Joy – "Hello Joy ... ju ... ju."

Joy tugs free, the leash slips from my hand and he bounds towards Rami. He wraps himself around his legs and puts his paws on his shoulders. Romi feeds him a well Juttered slice of bread lovingly and asks me anxiously, "Daddy, you're going to take Joy for his shots today, aren't you?" This is just an excuse to begin a conversation with me.

I nod in reply; I am not prepared for this query.

"What a long time you take to return!" Rama finds it necessary to say something as she shells a boiled egg.

"We have to leave early so we started breakfast," Archana says without raising her head.

"You should be careful about taking Joy out so early in the morning, people drive so recklessly."

I sit down in my chair and turn my plate over. Now what were the precautions the doctor had asked me to take? I try to remember.

"Poor thing ... How hungry he is! He has tired himself out Completely ... Listen, give him some milk, first." Archana wants

117

everyone to talk about Joy because she doesn't want anyone to talk about her.

The doctor has told me to take two pills before breakfast, but I am too exhausted to fetch them from my bedroom.

"You aren't going to skip your breakfast again today, are you?" Rama looks at me with exasperation.

"Okay, okay, I'll have my breakfast right away."

"Joy ... Joy ... ju ... ju" – Archana is playing with Joy. He touches her and then runs away, pulls at her saree, jumps up on to the sofa and then down.

The phone begins to ring. Joy stops playing and starts barking. Since he has to be quiet during phone calls, he hates them.

The call is for Romi – he signals Joy to be quiet – "Ushh ... Ushh!" Joy becomes silent but can hardly keep still. He begins searching the room for things he thinks are useless. First he picks up Archana's book and puts it in the dustbin. Then it is the turn of my medicine packet, then the flower from Rama's hair meets the same fate.

"Joy, put that in the dustbin too ... Distraught, I look up anxiously at Archana – she is pointing towards me – no, it isn't me, she is asking Joy to pick up a piece of bread lying next to my feet.

"Why don't you have your breakfast?" Rama is getting agitated.

"Yes, I will, but first I have to take my pills."

"You've spoilt your digestion by taking so many pills," she makes a face and leaves the table.

Joy picks up Romi's cigarette case and moves towards the dustbin but Romi puts down the phone and snatches it from his mouth. Be utters an obscenity and smacks him.

"If you ever touch any of my things again, I'll kill you and throw you into this very dustbin!"

The slap has left Joy stunned and the abuse has frightened him.

He comes towards me haltingly and lies down at my feet, panting.

Rama cannot bear to see Joy being hit but she does not dare open her mouth in front of her angry son.

"Why do you do such things to Joy?" Archana is indignant. "A rebuke would have been enough, no? Why should you hit him, as though he were a human being? What was the need to strike him?"

How well acquainted everyone is with Joy's nature, everyone of them is sympathizing with him because he is in pain – Joy, you are lucky indeed!

Before leaving home, every member of this house spends a long time before the mirror. Each one of them carefully puts on a mask, then sets out smiling to make this world their own, hoping to encash their cleverness. To achieve this, it is necessary to know how to act and also to put on good make-up.

"Joy ... ju ... ju ... ," Romi tries to appease Joy. Usually he would rush at Romi's call and keep jumping up and down until Romi's car disappeared at the gate. But today he just opens an eye, looks at him and turns his face away.

I begin to have a suspicion. Joy is acquiring a human soul! Gradually he is metamorphosing into a human being. If this really happens, he'll be thrown into a dustbin!

I begin to doze while reading the newspaper ...

I am lying under the table moaning with pain after Romi's slap. I have a chain around my neck which is being pulled by Joy.

"How cruelly you drag him ... " Rama says to Joy, "come, come my pet, come to my lap."

I jump into Rama's lap. She runs her fingers through my hair lovingly, and tears well up in my eyes.

I wonder who is weeping. Is it Joy, or is it me?

JOGINDER PAUL

KHODU BABA'S TOMB

TRANSLATED BY GILLIAN WRIGHT

$\mathscr{J}$oginder Paul was born in 1925 in Sialkot, Pakistan. He has an MA in English. He was associated with the Ministry of Education in Kenya for many years before he returned to India, to become the principal of a post-graduate college in Maharashtra. His published works include three collections of short stories, *Khula, Khodu Baba ka Maqbara* and *Katha Nagar*, a novella, *Khwabrau*, and a novel, *Nadeed*. His stories and novels have been translated into various Indian and foreign languages. Joginder Paul lives in Delhi.

"Khodu Baba ka Maqbara" was first published in the Urdu journal *Iblagh*, Peshawar.

$\mathcal{K}$hodu Baba and evening entered the slum colony one after the 'Other. Evening was advancing by itself, shadow by shadow, when a well-fed dog looked at Khodu Baba and barked, as if to say "Come, follow me!"

It set off ahead of Khodu Baba, down several narrow lanes, between small huts and shacks, until it brought him to the door of a hut of note. The Baba called out, "Haq!" Was it to himself or to summon the owner of the hut? This annoyed the dog. "Wahun! Wahun!" he began to bark. "Baba, calling the Chaudhuri is my job!"

Now, from inside the hut, a voice called out. "I hear you, Bandhu!" And Rakha Chaudhuri came out, tugging at his salwar. As he approached them, it started sliding down again and Rakha stopped to tighten its string. "Who have you got hold of this time?" he asked.

Rakha Chaudhuri seemed to have several holes in his nose through which his voice leaked out and became nasal in places. "You can't make a baba of just anyone and bring him here. How can I give a home to each one of them? Tell me."

Haq: Truth, that is God.

Bandhu retreated a little in fear, lifted his head in Khodu Baba's direction and growled, "Tell him!"

But the Baba stood in silence, staring at Rakha Chaudhuri. "Why are you staring at me like that, Baban?" asked Chaudhuri, staring back, curling his moustache. "I am no one else but myself."

"No, Khodu, how does Khodu know who Khodu is?" Khodu Baba said from under his thick beard,.

"My name is not Khodu, Baban." Before Chaudhuri was able to vent his anger, the Baba suddenly cried "Haq!" and picking up a stone, he flung it at Chaudhuri's legs.

"Ar-re!" Chaudhuri leaped backwards only to stand stock-still, his eyes fixed on a scorpion squashed flat right in front of him.

"Baap-re!" he exclaimed. The man he had taken for a beggar, could he be a saint?

"You need a hut, Baban? I'll willingly give it to you. For a single jhuggi I usually take a full five hundred and five rupees. But if you give me even two hundred and five, it'll do."

"I have needlessly killed a creature, Khodu ..." Khodu Baba said remorsefully.

"My name ..." Chaudhuri wanted to tell the Baba that his name was not Khodu, but stopped himself. Instead, "Why grieve over a dead scorpion, Baban?" he said. "That which stings must be killed."

"Scorpions also say, those who kill must be stung."

Who knows what came over Bandhu just then, for he suddenly began to roll at the Baba's feet.

"Arre, go away, you son of a dog!" said Rakha Chaudhuri, raising his arm and advancing towards him. "Go, do your chowkidari!"

But Khodu Baba bent down affectionately, patted the dog's back, and before straightening up, picked up a handful of dust which he poured over his head.

Rakha Chaudhuri gazed at him in astonishment. Then, as the thought dawned on him that this was really some kind of miracle man, he put both hands to his breast in a gesture of reverence. "Baba, how will you bear a burden of two hundred and five rupees?" Fumbling with the string of his salwar, chuckling, he continued, "Let's not worry about money. Come inside. I shall give you the money which you may then put back into my hands. The truth is that, if he wants to, Rakha will give up his life for a trifle, but a jhuggi? Never! But first, come, please do me the honour of coming inside."

With his hands to his breast as before, Rakha Chaudhuri turned towards his door and with his tail up like Bandhu's, led the way. Behind them Bandhu stood on his hind legs and tried to hold his front paws to his chest just as his master had done. When he failed in his efforts, he produced a monosyllabic bark as if saying, "Haq!"

Rakha Chaudhuri had every intention of welcoming the Baba with the liquor he had brewed himself. Here's a faqir par excellence, he thought. He must be in the fourth or fifth heaven already. But if his eyes could roll a little higher, he would get to the seventh heaven, and then, turning to me would say, "Haq! Now tell me Khodu, what do you want?"

In his heart of hearts Chaudhuri had already started to ask boons of Khodu Baba. "What is there to ask for, Baban? Ram Charan's Wife eats my jalebis every day but still won't let me even touch her. If only she came round!" But when he put the glass of liquor in front of the Baba, the faqir called out, "Haq!" in a loud voice, and banged the glass on the ground, lacerating his hand in the process. Khodu Baba wiped his bleeding palm on his beard and was about to stand up When Chaudhuri threw himself at the Baba's feet, silently cursing Ram Charan's wife. If she had come straight to him, he would not have had to go through all this trouble.

Prostrate at the Baba's feet, Chaudhuri began to pick up the pieces of broken glass.

Khodu Baba had already settled himself comfortably again. "He who doesn't forgive, Khodu, cannot escape punishment for the sin he does not forgive."

Cheered, Chaudhuri brought from his cupboard a bagful of jalebis that he had kept aside for Ram Charan's wife. The bitch had never responded to his love. He could at least earn a few blessings for himself from the Baba.

"Have some jalebis, Baban."

Khodu Baba brushed aside the bag. "No, sweets make you drowse and dream."

"Drowse and dream!" repeated Chaudhuri in admiration, kissing his fingertips as if he were kissing Khodu Baba's words.

"If you can, Khodu, in Allah's name, feed me a dry roti ..."

Chaudhuri had kept aside two or three rotis for Bandhu. But Bandhu will manage to pick a roti from somewhere, Chaudhuri thought. He took out the rotis wrapped in a piece of cloth, placed them in front of the Baba, and stood up to fetch a glass of water.

"Only one," the Baba took out one roti and held it in his hand.

"Are you sure I'm not depriving your Bandhu of his food?"

"Nothing is hidden from you, Baban. If you wait a little, I can get fresh rotis made for you in a minute."

"No, make fresh ones for Bandhu, Khodu."

Khodu Baba offered thanks to God and put the first morsel into his mouth.

"Shall I put a little salt on the roti, Baban?"

"Yes, Khodu, certainly, give me a little salt." For the first time the Baba laughed and it seemed to Chaudhuri that his hut was filled with light. The Baba added, "You know, for fear of being untrue to your salt, I shall always remember your kindness to me."

"No, Baban, don't say that," Chaudhuri placed a little pot of salt before the Baba. He was beginning to love his own modesty.

The Baba took a mouthful of water and stared in Chaudhuri's direction as if Chaudhuri was sitting behind himself.

Disconcerted, Chaudhuri turned back to reassure himself.

"Who are you looking at, Khodu?"

"Why, the one you are looking at, Baba. But I am here."

"Are you, Khodu?" The Baba murmured as he began to sprinkle salt on his roti.

"Only the Baban can understand the Baban," Chaudhuri comforted himself, asking aloud, "Baban, will you tell me something? Why do you call me Khodu?"

"Because I am also Khodu," replied the Baba, swallowing the morsel. "What do I possess in this world that I can give to anyone except my name? So that's why I give my name to everyone. Myself!"

Chaudhuri felt like stopping the Baba from eating, to kiss his fingers. "Baban," he said, "there is no scarcity of jhuggis here. Whichever you touch is yours. One of them has a very high roof. It's very spacious."

"No, I need the highest roof, the roof of the sky, Khodu," said the Baba, finishing the roti and wiping his hand on his beard. "I don't want any jhuggi-vuggi. If you give me a small open space, I'll settle there."

Chaudhuri decided that he would give the Baba the low brick platform a little distance away from the jhuggis on the edge of the burial ground. Into his good intentions, unknown even to himself, slipped a little bit of cunning: This way, it would also be easy to gain control over some of the cemetery land!

"Haq!" In a short while, the weary Baba's eyes became heavy and he began to stretch out where he sat.

"Wait, Baban, I'll spread out a sheet for you."

"No. Death may be of a moment or an eternity, but it must be on the bare ground. Haq!"

As soon as he lay down, the Baba began to snore.

Chaudhuri took the day's earnings out of his pocket and began to count them so that he could secretly put them away and go to sleep. "Haq!" Who was to know what he was trying to tell himself by calling out just like the Baba.

Who knows what kind of stories Rakha Chaudhuri had related to the people of the jhopadpatti! The very next evening, hordes of devout souls gathered at the Baba's chabootara.

The Baba was lying half supine on his platform, his back supported by a cushion of bricks. It looked as if a corpse, unable to endure the suffocation of the tomb, had come out into the open.

The Baba thought, the astonished people sitting near him appeared to him like shadows. He called out "Haq!"

Many people lifted their heads to the sky, as if his voice had descended from there. Some of them placed offerings in front of him.

The Baba noticed the edge of a dry roti peeping out of its newspaper wrapping. He bent forward, picked up the roti and began to eat it at once and in the time it took a man to run, fill a water jug, and return, the whole roti had disappeared into the Baba's stomach.

"Haq!" The Baba's mouth was still full of water.

As he spoke it was as if a natural spring had burst forth from behind a bushy thicket. His beard flooded, while the eyes of the faithful stayed fixed on him. The Baba" turned his back to the graveyard and bent over the other offerings. He held up a turban and gave it to a man whose head was bare.

"Take this, Khodu!"

He gave a jar full of pure honey to a wan-faced woman and, picking up a pair of shoes, he called to an old man with cracked feet – "Come, Khodu, take these!"

Badhwa Chamar stood up in indignation. "But I spent a whole good day making them for you, Baba. Such magic shoes that they fit any size!"

The old man, trembling with joy, quickly put on the shoes in case Badhwa made the Baba change his mind. "Baba, my daughterlaw always said, Why do you worry, Bapu? When you die, I'll send you from this world with shoes on." The old man wanted to break into a crazy dance.

Although the sky was quite clear, a few drops of water fell on the cheeks of the people, greatly refreshing them.

After the old man, the Baba called for Rakha Chaudhuri. "Take this," he said, giving Chaudhuri a fistful of dust from his chabootara.

Rakha took the dust and let it fall over his head just as the Baba had done.

Next, the Baba's eyes fell on a paper bag which contained laddoos. He was perhaps thinking of what should be done with them when it seemed as if he heard a voice behind him.

"Arre, hahn!" He turned ninety degrees. "Take these laddoos and share them amongst yourselves," he said, and dropped the bag of laddoos off the chabootara to his left.

Chaudhuri, peering in that direction, said, "But there's no one there, Baba."

"Reason blinds you, Khodu. Rub the dust well into your head and look. Who are those people sitting there - the old woman, the two young men and the three children?"

"Where?"

"Rub it in more. Those who come out of the grave can be seen with the head, not the eyes."

Perhaps all the people there had begun to use their heads, for they saw the six dead persons sitting on the edge of the cemetery. A few were scared, but what was there to fear when Khodu Baba was with them? They continued to sit where they were.

The Baba said, "You are all just as alive as you think you are. Tell me, am I right or wrong?"

"Absolutely right, Baban, absolutely right."

"If you love the dead, Khodu, they start breathing."

"Yes, Baba," said the wan-faced woman who had taken the jar of pure honey. "The Haji hakim told me, if I take honey, I'll live long."

A few young men had plucked up courage to move over and sit on the side of the graveyard.

"Well done! Always live together like this. And share whatever food you have among you!"

When it began to get dark Chaudhuri wanted to send a man to fetch a lantern. "No," the Baba scolded him. "Have you seen anyone except human beings lighting lamps, Khodu?" the Baba turned to the sky. "Look up there, see the lamps being lit, one after the other. Now, go home, all of you," he said, "Haq! Haq!"

His eyes were closed in full surrender even before he lay down.

Rakha Chaudhuri fell in behind everybody else and walked towards his hut. As he strolled slowly along, he watched the bandmaster and his wife walking hand in hand a little ahead of him. That's why when the bastard blows his trumpet the sound reaches the sky, he thought. And then he began to think again of his own Ram Charan's wife ...

The Baba is right. Share whatever food you have ... But Ram Charan's wife isn't an item of food and drink. And even if she were, she wouldn't come into my hands. Should I eat Ram Charan ... He persuaded himself to remove her from his heart. But he could do that only if she agreed to first set foot in it ... the face of Bebe Bashiran's widowed daughter began to swim before his eyes ... what a simple and humble woman she is! Why don't I ask Bebe for her hand? The very sight of her will make me observe the holy fast and say my prayers. She will turn me into another person. So what if she's forty? I've also left all my fifty years behind me ... it seemed he had made up his mind ... but there is one thing. Even though the widow pretends, if she wants to win my heart, then she has to keep on saying No, No, just like Ram Charan's wife ...

"Haq!" he cried out, happily and effortlessly.

The next day quite a few people again gathered at the chabootara.

"Ri, Shaidan!" Hirni saw her neighbour walking ahead of her and quickly caught up with her. "Are you also going to that Baba's tomb? You could have taken me too with you."

"Ashes in your mouth! Why say tomb? Say Baba's chabootara.

Yet ... " Shaidan halted a moment and looked in the direction of the platform, "it looks like a tomb."

"I say, Shaidan, these faqirs, they are very wise." Hirni's husband always said, My wife doesn't talk, she screams her way into your heart. "Even if dead, they can stand up again, brushing off their clothes. And if they feel like dying, they lie down wherever they like and start breathing their last, you know."

When they drew close to Khodu Baba, they halted, watchful. A canopy of innumerable yellow hornets hovered over the Baba's head.

"Don't be afraid, Khodu. They don't sting," he said, smiling. "Like You and me, they are happy just to buzz."

After a short while the buzzing canopy of hornets flew away from around the Baba's head and people came to settle down below the edge of the chabootara. A few sat on the near side and a few on the opposite side, close to the graveyard, where Khodu Baba had recognized several dead ones. "Arre, why are you all huddled together over here. Go there and sit with those people."

The Baba's eyes met Chaudhuri's. "Well, Chaudhuri, are you enjoying yourself?" Without waiting for a reply, he went on, "But how can you be enjoying yourself? When a person lives under such a big roof all alone, what alternative does he have? Tossing and turning in his grave, he cannot but turn his body round and round."

"We sleep so soundly in our graves that we have no idea what's going on in the world."

The Baba turned towards the speaker. "I'm talking of Chaudhuri. Your grave leaves you no space even to turn on your side."

"I have decided," said Chaudhuri in his nasal voice. "I shall celebrate my marriage the very next month."

"You will marry the girl who longs to drown in the music of your nose," said Bebe Bashiran who had also come there that day.

Everyone began to laugh.

It struck Chaudhuri that success might elude him here too. He resolved to go to Bebe Bashiran's jhuggi the very next day with some hot jalebis. Just a few sweet words would soften her. As for her widowed daughter, Sitara, poor thing, she was as meek as a cow. What was it to her if someone spoke through his nose or through his left or right ear? After the marriage he would bring Bebe Bashiran also to live with him. What would the old woman do alone in her jhuggi? Here she could look after the housework ... And her jhuggi, it is a very special jhuggi, he thought, it could be sold with all its furniture ... As he estimated the price it would fetch, he forgot all about Bebe Bashiran's widowed daughter. A full three thousand and five rupees ... maybe eighteen hundred or two thousand and five!

His eyes suddenly met Khodu Baba's. It seemed to him that the Baba had guessed his mind. He immediately decided that he would spend every paisa from the amount he received from the sale of Bebe Bashiran's jhuggi to build the Baba a first-class tomb. He would have a marble headstone put on the grave and inscribe on it some moving verses in the Baba's name which he would get his poet friend Suraj Narain Zakhmi to compose. Having rehearsed the whole scheme in his mind, he smiled – as did the Baba who was watching him steadily, as if the same thought had occurred to him simultaneously.

That day, Pandit Murlidhar was there, too, for a darshan of Khodu Baba. The Pandit had taken control over three jhuggis. He had knocked two of them into one and ran his preaching business from there. The third he had chosen for his residence. To one side of him sat a bald individual with a white moustache whom he had never seen before. The Pandit asked, laughing, "Well Bade Bhai, are you from our jhuggis over here or ..." gesturing towards the graveyard, "from over there?"

Such a strange laugh issued from the moustached man's throat that the Pandit was disconcerted and moved a little away from him.

Khodu Baba had overheard the Pandit's question. From the Pandit's choti and tilak he recognized him to be a Brahmin. Khodu Baba said:

"Paridit Khodu, when the path of knowledge distances us from others, we should take the road of blind faith, shouldn't we?"

"Yes, Baba," the Baba's attention went to the Pandit's head. As if to declare his faith in the Baba, he loosened his hair from its tightly-bound choti, folded his hands and said, "Your words have indeed made me happy."

"Haq!" Khodu Baba sat up straight. "Do you think I'm some kind of an entertainer, Khodu? I was not speaking to amuse you, Understand me, experience me."

The Pandit's face fell.

"Open your folded hands, Pandit Khodu. Now tell me," the Baba said, "who is greater, your simple, innocent mother who gave you birth or you with your great big choti?"

"My mother, generous one."

"In the very same way your simple, straightforward words are greater than all the secrets of your priestly trade ... here, let me tell you a tale, showing how deep are things that appear shallow."

"Wahun! Wahun!" Chaudhuri's guard dog came racing towards them. "Wait, Baba, let me sit down before you start your story."

"Yes, come Khodu, sit down, and listen carefully. It's a story about one of your own race."

Casting a glance over all those around him, the Baba said:

"Haq! Listen. There was in a very big town a smallish dog which used to wander aimlessly through the streets."

"Wahun!" Bandhu began to bark. "Who told you my story, Baba?"

"Arre, quiet!" said the Pandit, getting annoyed, his hands rising automatically to tighten the choti on his head. "Listen quietly!"

"Haq!" the Baba paused. Then he said, "He was an unfortunate street dog. Had he been a pet, he would have been fed on bread and butter and 'meat just for running to catch the ball his master had thrown. Not only that, whenever his master and mistress quarrelled, he would have found space in her bed to lick her and cuddle against her."

"Wahun!" Bandhu couldn't bear to keep quiet. "You're quite right, Baba."

"Ane, again!" Now the Pandit tightened his choti with such ferocity that Bandhu could not help yelping.

"If you love your life, Bandhu, then don't interrupt," said Bebe Bashiran, taking pity on the dog. "Even our Bade Maulvi is scared of the Pandit's choti."

"Haq! Listen on ... he who has no name may have several names or just this one – Khodu. And so this street dog whom the world called by any name that came to mind, was known in the butchers' market as Khodu Dulla. Sometimes he would keep his eye on the crows and pariah kites in front of one shop, and then another. In return for this voluntary service, the butchers would throw him a few bones and scraps before shutting shop. But one day he felt that out of the corner of their eyes, the butchers were measuring his neck and smiling. They were perhaps planning to mix his meat with the mutton. Scared, he stopped going to their side of town. Haq!"

Before proceeding to the next section of his story the Baba became quiet for a moment.

"Then it so happened that in one residential area he started an affair with a pet bitch."

Shaidan and Hirni could not contain their joy and surprise at this and tinkled like brass bells.

"This bitch would address our Khodu with great love and affection, as Wahun."

"Wahun!" Bandhu interrupted again, "Wahun is no name."

"My brother," Khodu Baba replied; "the bitch didn't know English to call him Tommy or Tiger. She addressed him simply in her native bark, her original language. She was the pet of a devout cloth merchant. Like her owner, she ate only chapatis, vegetables and

135

fruit and drank plain, clean water and, of course, participated in Hari Kirtan with the rest of the household."

"This is really most unusual, Baba," said the Pandit, happily impressed.

"Listen further. Khodu Wahun was on top of the world here. As evening deepened, he would slip out of sight, jump off the compound wall of the house and tiptoe to his beloved. Then, who knows who put the evil eye on her. The bitch suddenly died for no apparent reason."

"Wahun!" By now Bandhu had begun to think deeply of the bitch. "How could that happen? There must have been some reason?"

"There must have been. Anyway, Khodu eventually forgot the name his beloved had given him and went back to tread the city streets. He ate whatever he could find, or he barked out Allah's name and lay down wherever he found himself."

While this tale was being told, Bandhu saw a bitch in the graveyard and he left everything to leap away in her direction. All eyes followed him, but he had hardly come close to the bitch when he began to bark, turned tail and raced back.

"Wahun! That is Chhabeeli," he said, collecting himself, "the one who died more than three months ago."

"What's there to be afraid of?" the Baba began to laugh. "Poor creature, maybe she couldn't find a place to stay in after her death."

Bandhu looked back at the cemetery. At first hesitantly and then swiftly, he went towards her again.

"Your story, Baba?"

"The story continues ... Khodu managed to somehow survive for three or four months but how could he keep his four legs standing without food or drink? No one in the whole town had time to spare him a glance. He wandered around hiding his face because in big towns they shoot stray dogs."

"Then"

"Then happened what should have happened long before. One day Wahun ... "

"But he has no name now, remember ... "

"Yes, now he is plain Khodu ... so one day, Khodu dropped dead in the street. But no one had any idea who had died or if anyone had died at all. In that busy market, he lay dead for days. No one noticed him. People notice you only when you are someone."

"But Baba," Bandhu asked from where he sat with Chhabeeli, at the edge of the cemetery, their legs entwined – they had rediscovered their relationship in that short time – "aren't poor dogs also human?"

"Yes, Bandhu, if anyone takes them as such," said the Pandit answering instead of the Baba.

"But why don't they?" came the voice of the white-moustached man sitting by the Pandit. "We are humans. Yet we long for someone to think of us as their pets."

At this point some deep experience possessed the Baba. Suddenly oblivious of everyone, he shut his eyes and began to chant "Haq! Haq!" in a soft tone. His audience watched him in silence for a while. When he did not stir, they all stood up to go. Finding Bandhu still entwined with Chhabeeli, Chaudhuri swore at them and said, "Arre, get up! Is this the time for love-making or for chowkidari?"

The next evening too, at precisely the same time, many people gathered at Khodu Baba's low brick platform.

"You left yesterday's story unfinished, Baba." The Pandit had come that day as well.

"Stories are always unfinished," replied Khodu Baba, "because they are about the people who leave us saying they will be back soon;

137

but they never return. We wait for them but it's always someone else who comes."

"I don't understand, Baba," the man asking this question sold vegetables from a handcart and was bitter by nature. So he was known as karela or bitter gourd. "If my vegetables are not sold for a day, they begin to rot and smell. Your Wahun's corpse lay in such a busy street and no one smelt the rot?"

"In a busy street, hundreds of smells mix together, Khodu. So how does anyone know what smell is coming from where?"

The Baba suddenly noticed Bandhu sitting sadly apart from everyone else with his face towards the graveyard.

"The dead lady hasn't come today?"

"No, Baba, I don't know why."

"Who knows, perhaps she's not well."

"You say some very strange things, Baba. Once you're dead don't all diseases disappear?"

"If one can live after death, why can't one fall sick too?" Running his gaze over the crowd, the Baba was struck by a very beautiful, grubby girl. He paused to look at her but the girl thought that he was looking at the goat behind her which sat moving its jaws though its mouth was empty.

"This is Balo, my goat, Baba ... "

The Baba was about to reply when he saw, slouching in front of him, a toothless old woman whose dry dust-coloured face was crisscrossed by innumerable wrinkles, like lines and cracks on a piece of ancient drought-parched earth. She said, "I have an all-time fever."

"What fever ... Oh, an all-time fever."

The old woman untied the knot at the end of her coarse saree. "I have these tablets from the Khairati Dawakhana," she said, taking out a small packet and showing the Baba the pills inside. "But the doctor says I should have good food too."

It was as if fresh water from a well were pouring out of the Baba's eyes and flooding the parched drought-stricken earth. "Do you have anyone of your own, Mat"

The Pandit said, "Her own was only her own self. And how is even that her own, Khodu?"

The Baba beckoned to the goat-girl. Her goat too came running behind the girl.

"Will you do me a favour, Khodu?"

"Yes, Khodu Baba, whatever you say. Don't ask me to do just one thing - to get married."

"Why not?" asked the Baba with interest.

"Why should I? That man will snatch me from myself and my goat too."

Khodu Baba smiled. "Every day, give some of your goat's milk to this Khodu Ma. As a reward, Allah will send you a very special nawab bridegroom."

"Then tell your Khuda, Baba, to send two nawabs, not one. If one turns out to be worthless, there will be the second. Come, Ma, come to me every day for a paiya of fresh milk."

When she moved away, the Pandit said to the Baba, "So that Wahun of yours just lay on the footpath?"

"Yes, but one day, unable to bear his own stench, dead as he was, he stood up and headed out of the town, that he might find some plain ground, dig a hole, pull the mud on top of himself and lie there ... " Bandhu suddenly remembered something. "Baba," he asked, "did you dig the hole at the back of Chaudhuri's house?"

"Yes, Khodu, why? That night when I slept there, my eyes opened early in the morning. When I came out and my eyes fell on a spade, I couldn't contain myself. One man can lie down comfortably in it."

139

"But which man, Baba?"

"Why, anyone, even your Khodu Chaudhuri. I thought, when his time comes why should he roam from place to place? He has been so kind to me. I should also do him a good turn."

Rakha Chaudhuri, disconcerted, laughed loudly.

"Was Wahun successful in leaving the town?" asked the Pandit. "First, it so happened that trying to leave the city, he slipped even further into the city. Then one day discovering himself in the very innermost part of it, he suddenly found himself outside it. But what was the point? Wherever he started scraping the earth with his paws" the owner of the land would come running with a lathi in his hand," the Baba paused for a moment before continuing. "All the land had been allotted to various people. There was not even a foot left in Allah's name."

"What disaster befell Khuda that He had to sell all the land to those tyrants?"

"I don't know. But it must have been some real disaster. Otherwise, he would have retained at least a quarter if not a half in His own name."

Suddenly something came over the Baba. He put his arms down, hands to the ground, as if they were the forelegs of a dog and crawled around the chabootara once.

"Baaaa ...!"

"Quiet," said the beautiful girl, putting her hand over the goat's mouth. "I haven't brought you with me for this."

"Wahun! Wahun!" Bandhu addressed the Baba, "What is this drama, Baba? Finish your story."

"The story continues like this," said the Baba. "That son of a dog ran and ran until he came to a new settlement. He was beaten there, so he went to another. He ran around from place to place and in all the months and years of running, he even forgot that he was dead, that he was alive only by mistake," the Baba's voice seemed to fade away in the flood of his inner self. "But as he wandered, whenever he found the chance to sit in peace on plain earth, he would smile and automatically begin to scratch the earth, not knowing why he was doing it," the Baba had rested one hand in a small hole and buried his eyes into the several small holes on the platform which perhaps he had dug with his own nails.

"Arre, Baba, can I tell you something?" a young layabout couldn't keep quiet. "That son of a dog is no one else but you."

"Does the Baba look like the son of a dog to you?"

"If you are confronted with a mountain of troubles then the son of a dog can begin to look like a man."

"Wahun! Wahun!"

"Baaaa ... "

"Haq! Haq! Haq!"

That morning Koran Tai was to bring rotis for Khodu Baba at the chabootara.

Koran Tai used to leave her jhuggi at the break of dawn to sweep and dust ten houses from where she earned enough rotis and abuses to fill her stomach. When she finished her work, she would return to her jhuggi in the evening, light a clay lamp and stretch out on her cot as if she were laid out for her funeral rites.

She had said to the Baba the previous day, "Before I go to work, I'll bring some rotis for you. Eat them when you are hungry."

Khodu Baba was wondering why Tai was so late. Should he go to her jhuggi to find out? That moment, he saw Bandhu running towards the chabootara. In his mouth he was carrying a roti wrapped in a newspaper. Dropping it in front of the Baba, he said panting,

"Tai has vomitted blood. Wahun! I was going past her jhuggi when she said, I have already made a roti for the Baba but I am not able to walk up to him. You give it to him. And give my Ram, Ram too, to Allah's good man."

"May Allah be merciful to her!" Khodu Baba said softly as he took the roti in his hand. Tai had very thoughtfully spread chutney over it.

"Haq!"

"Wahun! She's a good woman, Baba, and very unhappy," Bandhu felt like running off, barking loudly. "If you can't free her of her pain, Baba, what is the point of being such a great faqir? Wahun!"

"The point comes only from simple and ordinary people." Khodu Baba rolled up the roti, bit off a mouthful and began to chew it. "A wretched faqir is only concerned about himself, foolish Khodu!"

"Wahun! Look, Baba, either call me a fool or Khodu."

"They both mean the same, foolish one," the Baba laughed, "Watch over Tai, Khodu."

"I do watch, but how can I watch over the whole lot of them? Every single life hangs by a thread."

Bandhu began to tell the Baba about various people living in the slum.

"That old man you gave Budhu Chamar's shoes to, he is on his deathbed. Since last night he has been saying to his son again and again, Let me leave this world with my shoes on or I'll come back and haunt you."

As if he had made up his mind to ask the Baba this question, Bandhu asked, "Baba, don't you feel afraid at night, all alone in this deserted graveyard?"

"Afraid of what?"

"Wahun! Of ghosts, Baba, what else?"

"You are not afraid of ghosts either, Khodu."

"No, Baba, I'm very afraid."

"Then ... "

Bandhu looked into the Baba's eyes and although he tried to stop himself, he began to bark.

"You are a fool of fools, Khodu."

"No, Baba, you are not a ghost, and even if you are, how can I be afraid of you? You are my own Baba!" As if he had suddenly remembered something, he started to say, "Do you know what? Yesterday Uchit Seth – he is the poorest of them all, so Abdul Chacha jeeringly calls him Uchit Seth. He 'has rented his jhuggi from Abdul Chacha but never pays the rent – Uchit Seth came here last evening to hear you speak. When he went back he gulped down a whole half-bottle of country liquor outside his doorstep, and forced me to sit with him, and said, Listen, Khodu. That miserable cur about whom Khodu Baba was telling the story, do you know who he is? Me ... I am that son of a dog. Look at me. And, like you, Baba, he put both his hands to the ground and began to bark so loudly that even when I joined in the barking, I could hear just him. What dog is he whose bark cannot be heard, Baba?"

Perhaps to overcome his embarrassment, Bandhu began to bark so loudly that the Baba warned him to quieten down.

"Achcha, I'll speak softly. Uchit Seth says that we are all our own ghosts, who, unable to bear our own stench after death, stand up on all fours. You won't believe, Baba, he even told me the date of his death. He's a deeply unhappy man. He drinks to forget his pain but When he's drunk his troubles come to his mind even more." The dog's wahun-wahun began to grow louder with anger and grief. "Last year his wife died of - what do you call that disease – syphilis. Yesterday when he was fully drunk, he asked me, How can I mourn for my wife? I died four years before her, the day a tourist asked me to bring him a well-built young woman and I persuaded my own wife, dressed her, and took her to him. If there's money in the house what else do you need? ... He began to cry, Baba, and asked, Don't I appear to you as a ghost of myself? I blinked rapidly as I looked at him. Sometimes I could see all of him clearly and sometimes only his nose, mouth or eyes appeared on his face. I got frightened and ran away from there," Bandhu gave a few quick yaps.

"Wahun! Why have you stopped eating?" Bandhu asked the Baba. "For one thing, you never eat your fill, and what you do eat is so little – as little as the chowkidari I pretend to do. Shall I tell you the truth? My stomach doesn't get full with Rakha Chaudhuri's two rotis. I am always on the lookout to steal something from every jhuggi and now I shall have to work even harder for Chhabeeli. Where has this Chhabeeli disappeared for the last couple of days, Baba? I think that the news of her death was a hoax. She must have gone back to some lover of hers. She must have had a fight with him and come here. Now that her temper's cooled down, she's gone back to him. She uses me as a cover for honour and propriety. That's all. I wish she had stayed dead! ... ha ... ha ... Wahun!" All of a sudden Bandhu's anger turned into laughter.

"What is there to laugh at, Khodu?"

"There is, Baba, there is! I was thinking of Ram Charan's wife," Bandhu held himself from laughing. "Last night Ram Charan's wife ran away with the milkman, Janglu. Rakha Chaudhuri had his eyes on her, Baba. This morning when I went to Chaudhuri's house, he started abusing me for no reason at all. He rained stones on me. I too lost my temper and barked ferociously. At last he calmed down and begged forgiveness and said, Am I even worse than Janglu? Tell me the truth, he insisted. Now what could I say? Today he's put on new clothes and gone to Bebe Bashiran's with a basketful of jalebis."

Khodu Baba chuckled.

"Always laugh like this, Baba," said Bandhu wagging his tail with delight. "I like you this way."

Bandhu saw that directly opposite him, beneath a keekar tree, a black cobra, half inside its hole, was watching the Baba, swaying and hissing delightedly.

"Why does your breath dry at the sight of him? He too is a good friend, Khodu." Stuffing the last mouthful of roti into his mouth, the Baba stood up. "Come, let's go and see Tai. We can as well drink water there."

Without answering, the frightened Bandhu turned immediately and ran off ahead of the Baba.

"Slowly, Khodu, slowly! Walk along with me."

"Seeing that friend of yours nearly took my life away."

"In spite of that, you're running around – Haq!"

Bandhu turned his head to measure the distance between himself and the keekar tree and then, as something occurred to him, he stopped. "There is a very good Christian woman in our slum colony, Baba – Rosy Mother. She wants to meet you tomorrow. Since she Works in the evening, she can only come during the day."

"What does she do?"

"She sells her body."

Bandhu looked back and was about to run ahead when the Baba Warned him again, "Slowly!"

"I can't go slowly, Baba," Bandhu replied before starting to run again, "You may walk on slowly. I'll go and tell Tai."

The next day when Rosy Mother came to the Baba's chabootara, she immediately presented him with two apples which the Baba took in his hands and then returned to her. "When you leave here, give these apples to Khodu Tai."

"Who is Khodu Tai?" Mother asked, then said with a laugh, "Achcha, our Tai Koran. No problem at all. I'll give the apples to her." Then she took a bottle of foreign liquor from her bag. "But this, Tai Koran won't take."

"Haq!" the Baba's face lit up with rage.

Mother quickly put the bottle back into her bag and despite being scared, her voice was sharp, "What do you think, Baba, that I like this way of life? But if I don't do this, what do I do? You're a man of God, Baba. How can I hide anything from you?" she began to speak freely. "Just think! At my age, should I entrust my body to a customer or to God Almighty? Tell me, Baba. Sometimes when I am in the arms of a strong, young man, I think of my dead son and cry," there was a tone of pleading insistence in her voice. "I loathe myself, Baba, then why do you also hate me?"

Rosy Mother's honest confession had softened the Baba. "Tell me, what do you want from me?"

"What else can I want? I've heard that when you call them, the dead come back to life," Mother's eyes were bright with tears. "Let me meet my Vicky just once."

Khodu Baba felt as if Mother Rosy's heart were beating in his own breast. "I shall let you meet him – Haq! – I will surely do so."

Mother was confused. How was the Baba going to do that?

"My Vicky died a whole year ago, Baba."

"So what, Mother? Just because a poor man dies, he is not always delivered from life."

That evening practically the entire population of the slum colony had gathered at the Baba's chabootara. Even the far side of the graveyard was fully occupied. Who knows how many ghosts and inmates of the graveyard had also found places to sit there!

As on the first day, Khodu Baba lay half reclining, his back supported by the pile of bricks at one end of the chabootara, absolutely still, staring at the sky with wide open eyes as if he had just risen from his grave and, even as he lay there lifeless, had reached the heavens in search of himself.

Everyone was singing the Baba's praises, but their ears were alert for the moment when he would say "Haq!" so they could immediately turn their attention to him.

Finding the Baba in this state, Pandit Murlidhar reverently untied the knot of his hair. "I have seen great faqirs and mahatmas, Chaudhuri," he said to Rakha Chaudhuri, who was sitting next to him, "but our Baba Khodu has absolutely no equal."

"Is that why it's taking him so long to get back?" Rakha Chaudhuri was worried why Khodu Baba had not yet come back to the present.

"Did you hear?" the Pandit interrupted him. "Someone laughed!"

"So what, Pandit? Can't anyone laugh without getting you to perform a puja first?"

"No, Chaudhuri," said the Pandit, lowering his voice to emphasize his point, "I don't mean these people ... listen, someone laughed again ... I mean those people ..." He gestured towards the graveyard.

"So what?" asked Chaudhuri, imitating the Baba. "Whether from this side or that, all God's creatures are equal."

"Look, Baba has begun to stir."

Chaudhuri immediately looked at the Baba, "That's a fly hovering over the Baban's mouth," he rose and went close to the Baba to brush the flyaway. He suddenly shouted, "Oh, you fools," everyone jumped and began to look in his direction, "the Baban is not here."

"So who is it lying in front of us?" asked the Pandit.

"The Baban has already left us."

"Wahun! Wahun!" Bandhu also came up and stood, barking, by the Chaudhuri. "Wahun!"

"Do not be afraid," said the Pandit, as everyone jumped to their feet. "Wherever he's gone, he'll come back in a short while." Again it seemed as if several of the dead burst out laughing in unison. The Pandit was unnerved. "Look carefully, Chaudhuri," he called out. "Are you sure the Baba hasn't passed away?"

"Yes, Shaidan," Hirni was telling her neighbour, "pirs and faqirs are never where they seem to be, you know. Who knows where these men of Khuda leave their bodies and go?" And finding the attention of all the others on herself, she got carried away by her own words. "I am not comparing myself with the Baba. Where is Baba, and where a great fool like me? Yet so many times I've felt that though I'm stuck here in Chaudhuri's slum colony, I am playing adi tappa in my mother's courtyard. So, tell me, where am I really? If I have to search for myself where should I look?"

"Wahun!" Bandhu, looking dejected, stood before them, barking.

"Sit down comfortably. Wahun!"

"So Hirni," Shaidan was saying, "before the Baba came wandering to this place, where was he lying, just like this?"

"Wahun!" said Bandhu, and to address them all, he came and stood on the chabootara next to Khodu Baba. "In the past the Baba wandered everywhere in search of a place to settle. Wahun! Now he doesn't have to go anywhere. Wahun! He has settled here for ever. Wahun! Wahun!"

"Haq!"

❦ MOHAMMAD MANSHA YAD ❧

FIREFLIES IN A CLENCHED FIST

TRANSLATED BY RASHID

$\mathcal{M}$ohammad Mansha Yad was born in 1937 in Sekhpura district, now in Pakistan. After a diploma in Civil Engineering, he joined an organization which was formed specifically to supervise the construction and development of Pakistan's new capital, Islamabad, where he settled in 1963. Mansha Yad has an MA in Urdu and Punjabi. He started writing short stories and poems for children's magazines at a very young age. His first story was published in 1955. His published works since then include his collections of stories, *Band Mutthi Mein Jugnu, Maas aur Mitti, Khala Andar Khala;* and in Punjabi, *Wagdha Paani*, which received the Waarish Shah Award from the Academy of Pakistan. He has also written features for radio and television. Mohammad Mansha Yad lives in Islamabad.

"Band Mutthi Mein Jugnu" is the title story from his first collection of stories, published in 1975.

When the women in the neighbourhood started fighting, she was all alone in the house. She had not brought any books or magazines with her from the city. She was weary of them. But she had wiped and dusted Sharif's old and torn class VIII books several times since the morning.

Sharif and Bablu had gone to bring Sharifan back from Chacha's village. Sharifan was not in the house but she could smell her fragrance on every object, in every corner. And she herself? She was there, yet it seemed as if she was not.

A short while ago, before going to the field with the lunch, Phuphi had loaded her with a sack of loneliness. If those women had not started quarrelling, she would have had to touch herself again and again, to assure herself that she was actually there.

Lying beneath that burden of loneliness, she felt almost as if she Was being being engulfed by its stale, musty smell. Just then, the clouds began to roar and big streams of sound fell on the still waters of silence. Those were the last few days of July. The real clouds and the real sun were at a game of hide-and-seek, the sun's long tongues of flame licking the damp off the emaciated, surma-dark clouds.

In her childhood, she used to think that there were countless suns in the sky and that every day a new sun appeared. For a long time she had believed that every night one sun was put out, and that the next morning another sun, similar, but bigger or smaller depending on the season, rose. She had loved them all- the living, blazing ones as well as the dying, setting ones. Even the broken heaps of these fading suns were useful, for angels picked up their pieces and, after polishing them, made them rise into the night as the moon. But now she knew that it was the same old sun and the same tired moon being used every day.

She was so tired of old things.

There was a universal shortage of freshness. Every morning weak cows of decay swallowed the plump cows fed on freshness. Away from the rays of the sun, freshness was stored in the refrigerator for many, many days. Freshness was sold in the market like eight-day-old dead fish. To hide the decay of the body, each day new fashions came up and the old was given a coating of gilded words.

Simulated fights on television and in films were as dull as oft-repeated jokes. She reflected for a while on the originality of the fights of village women, and then extricating herself from the sack of silence, started going up the stairs one by one.

It was truly a fierce fight. Loud voices exploded like cannons in the far distance.

Ttha ... ttha ... ttha ...

She sat down on the last step and took a long, deep breath. A feeling of freedom and freshness crept into her. She wanted to stand on the hen coop and call out to all those miserable people far away who were trying to peck their way out of their own eggs, just like live young chicks.

The fighting women's faces were flushed with anger but not disfigured with hate. Their voices had the crackle of lightning, not the hiss of snakes. Among those women, she recognized Nooran and Mahran. Sharifan often talked about them and last evening they had even come to meet her, but now she knew that both of them were mere clever scandalmongers.

If only she too were a scandalmonger!

One gets so tired of living with the same name all the time, trapped in the same role, the body stained by grease and dirt and the mind gnawed by termites of monotony.

When he went to offer Eid prayers at the mosque, Abba would go by one road and come back by another. By taking a new path, one gets greater rewards in the next life.

But she did not ever change her route to college. Year after year, she repeated the same notes, the same texts, the same lectures. While reiterating the golden sayings of great philosophers, she would feel ashamed as if she were making her class memorize the multiplication table of two.

Sometimes her voice got stuck in the throat and she would feel there was a grinding stone on her shoulders instead of her head. The bright sun before her eyes would begin to fade. She would feel nauseous and faint, and only when she regained her senses would she realize that she had had a seizure.

She had, in fact, advised herself to come and stay with Sharifan for a few days. Ever since college closed, her mind was always caught in little whirls. Even if she did not want to think, tough-bodied bandicqots of thought, continuously screaming, burrowed into her mind.

The quarrelling women were divided into two distinct camps, supporting either the Jethani, the older sister-in-law, or the Devrani, the younger one. Each side had one old woman and three or four younger ones. While the knight took on the knight, the pawns were fighting pawns.

The young ones seemed as if they were fettered by big dreams.

Dreams?

Heaviness in the stomach?

Wandering thoughts?

Unknown desires?

Once, while making tea, she saw herself trapped in the kettle. She screams and shouts but no one removes the lid. She suffocates and dies. She often wondered whether that was just a dream, whether she wasn't really dead. She kept touching herself everywhere to see if she was alive or not.

Even in a house full of people, loneliness and melancholy were stretched around her like a tent. Sometimes she would open the unread book of her body and sit herself down to look at the images, but then quickly put it away for fear that it might get dirty.

And when she had to repeat the multiplication table hundreds of times, everything would appear stale. Her own body, which she had thought had a golden sheen, would start to look like dry leather. Her sweat would smell of dead fish and when she opened magazines or books, she would see dead flies stuck here and there.

When she sat idle, thoughts, like odious bats, flapped about in her mind and everything seemed repulsive. Music sounded like a hundred crows cawing together over a dead crow. Eggs smelt of chicken shit, rotis of sawdust, and meat of dead flesh. Waves of stench enveloped her, her stomach churned and she would start vomiting.

The women in the Jethani's group were chudails, dayans and hogs, who sucked blood, devoured hearts and wove all kinds of spells.

Those in the Devrani's camp were tough and cunning, with roving eyes and wanton looks, leading a thoroughly dissipated life.

She was so envious of them.

She did not find anything wrong with throwing wanton glances, casting spells and romping with a lover. Her mind was clouded in the truth of this sweltering sunshine .

The Jethani's hens had got into the habit of laying their eggs in the Devrani's house and then going, clucking, to Jethani's to roost. But Devrani's claim was that these shameless hens laid no eggs, clucked to conceal their barrenness, and crowed every morning, like roosters.

She could not understand many things because of their specific geographical and historical references. But it did not take long for the subject matter to change, and the volley of words they used made their arguments very colourful. Where can one find such unusual examples of fabrication and transgression in books! However, in spite of the striking originality in their use of metaphors, it was turning into empty rhetoric.

Everyone at home took care to see that nothing upset her. But the people in the city did not know that in her a life-size instrument has been created to identify old, worn-out ideas and to point to obsolete and barren ones with a hundred per cent efficacy.

Under the pretext of the fight, seven previous generations of the warring groups were being invoked. Was there any point in digging up old graves? Who knows! And if there was, who knows if the bodies were properly shrouded or not. She remembered stories about naked women dancing around a bonfire in the graveyard. And she felt like going to the graveyard secretly, one night.

The quarrelling women had now got out of the quagmire of taunts and stepped into the deep waters of obscenities. It was for the first time in her life that she was hearing such stark naked abuses. When she heard all the parts of the human body being mentioned, her mind opened up and suddenly, all the little birds caged inside flew away. One by one, the leeches that had been sticking to her body for so long, started to fall off. And gradually, a new sun began to rise within her. Her body began to glow from its rays. Her face flushed with a delicious warmth. She was drenched in perspiration. For the first time she found her sweat smelled like roses. Her body seemed weightless and was rising above the ground.

At that instant, Sharifan arrived.

Sharifan's expansive presence pervaded the whole house. Lured by the magnetism of her body and drawn by the string of her voice, she came back to earth.

The battle was in full swing when suddenly, a danger siren sounded. Men entered the houses, and spears and lances began to glint and flash. She froze with fear. A fight amongst men looks good only on the cinema screen.

At that very moment, Allah sent down an angel of mercy. A man of around sixty or seventy years, with a gentle bearing and an infinitely wise face, came in and stood between the two groups like a wall of reconciliation and peace. Sharifan told her that the man she had mistaken for an angel was Ahmed Din Teli. She did not believe it until they pushed him aside roughly. Yes, he was Ahmed Din Teli.

Seeing the attempts at peace fail, her heart started thudding. She shuddered as she visualized intestines hanging out of ripped bellies and headless bodies writhing. But then something strange happened.

A puny, feeble-looking man came in and started hurling vulgar abuses at them. As soon as they saw him, the tensed necks and raised spears slackened and drooped. One by one the women and children slipped away from the rooftops. In no time the battleground was calm, cool as a block of ice.

She was totally bewildered.

She began to feel like a firefly in a closed fist. Ugly thought-rats began to bury their snouts into her mind and shriek.

Hundreds of naked village children surrounded her, reciting the two-times table. Filthy flies swarmed around her. The stench of burning flesh spread all around. She was suffocating under the grinding stone. She tried to breathe in fresh air but a host of buzzing flies were stuck in her throat. She began to vomit.

☙ QURRATULAIN HYDER ☙

HONOUR

TRANSLATED BY THE AUTHOR

Qurratulain Hyder was born in Aligarh and educated in Lucknow, from where she got her Master's degree in English literature. Both her parents were well-known literary figures. Her father was one of the founders of the modern Urdu short story and her mother was an eminent popular novelist of her time. Qurratulain Hyder has published several collections of short stories and a number of novels. Many of her books have been translated into Indian and foreign languages. She has received a large number of literary awards, including India's most prestigious literary award, the Jnanpith, in 1990. She has worked in England as a journalist and has travelled widely all over the world. She is at present a Fellow of the Sahitya Akademi. Though she is an innovator in modern Urdu fiction, the present story has been written in the traditional narrative style. Qurratulain Hyder lives in Delhi.

"Hasab Nasab" has been published in *Azadi ke Baad Dilli Mein Urdu Afsana*, The Urdu Academy, Delhi.

*T*he bathroom was like the cave of the Forty Thieves – dark, damp, cool and full of massive gleaming things such as hamams, engraved washbasins and tall brass jugs with slender spouts. The clotheshorses looked like mysterious brigands. Shamshad Begum had to make her way through all this before she could get to the window. She had scraped a little paint off one of the panes so that she could watch her rakish, handsome fiance flitting in and out of the outer courtyard. Once Shah Jahan gazed like this at the Taj from the window of the palace where his son held him captive.

The window overlooked the adjoining house. Its walled front garden was lined with jasmine and pomegranates and had a fountain in the middle. This house came to be known as the Chameliwali Haveli. It was the domain of Aziz Khan, the cousin whom Shamshad Begum was to marry. Once in a while, Aziz Khan, affectionately called Ajju Bhai, sauntered down to the main entrance of the zenana and shouted – in a special tone of voice meant only for her – "I say, will someone send us more tea and hot pakoras." That was enough. Shamshad ran hotfoot to the kitchen across the spacious zenana courtyard. Aziz

Khan would return to his cronies and his pigeons and his paper kites. He was an only son and had been thoroughly pampered by his parents. And Shamshad, better known as Chhami Begum, adored him.

They led a peaceful life in Shahjahanpur. Their ancestors, like the other Rohilla Pathans, had come many centuries ago from Afghanistan. An entire region in the western United Provinces was named Rohilkhand after them.

Chhami Begum lived in a traditional joint family. Both her father and his cousin were landowners.

The Pathans of Rohilkhand were proud of their Afghan ancestry. They had retained their pink-and-white complexion, robustness and good looks. Chhami Begum was tall and pretty. She lived in strict purdah, had never been to school and had been taught Urdu, Arabic and Persian at home. She too was an only child.

The marriage date had been fixed when disaster struck. Cholera broke out in Shahjahanpur. Within a few days, both her parents were dead. Chhami was stunned. She was consoled by her future parents-in-law. The wedding was postponed. It was a long time before she went back to gaze out of the green window.

One night Aziz's father had a heart attack. He died within a few hours. Chhami began to believe that she was an abhagin, the unfortunate one. After some days, Ajju Bhai told his mother that he had to attend to some court cases in Allahabad. As affluent landowners they were forever involved in litigation, a favourite pastime of both her father and her uncle.

Ajju Bhai went away to Allahabad. In the autumn afternoon, the wind rustled in the empty, walled garden. Everybody had suddenly vanished: Abbu, Chachajan, Ajju Bhai. A year went by and Ajju Bhai did not come back. Chhami took to hiding in the dark bathroom where she buried her face in soft muslin dupattas, stacked on a clotheshorse, and cried.

It was uncanny. Chachijan, her aunt, followed her husband. She died of pneumonia. But Chhami knew that, more than pneumonia, it was a broken heart.

After her father's death Chhami Begum had become heir to a vast fortune with Ajju Bhai as her legal guardian. Where was he? Lucknow ... Calcutta ... Mussoorie ... Nainital? The rumours said he was busy squandering the money that had come to him after his father's death. Chhami Begum was then a minor. In the absence of Ajju Bhai, her other relatives cheated her of most of her inheritance.

The years went by with amazing speed. She was thirty ... and still waiting for Ajju Bhai. She had been an arrogant young girl ... age and misfortune had mellowed her. But she remained inordinately proud of her family. A noble Rohilla maiden, she would remain true to the pledge her Abba had given his cousin ... she was after all the only remaining custodian of the family honour ...

Chhami's hair turned grey. She locked herself inside the haveli and stopped meeting people. Every Friday she went to the men's quarters and had the place swept, the rooms aired and the Victorian furniture dusted. She tended the trees and flowering shrubs in the courtyard and cleaned the fountain clogged with yellow leaves. He might turn up any time ... you never know.

In the heavy silence of long summer afternoons, she lay on a divan in the arched verandah, dozing or staring at the tamarind which towered above the zenana courtyard. Salamat, the old cook, sat on a cot under the tree, chewing tobacco. Often, she muttered to herself. "Allah Mian laughs only twice: once when He bestows honours on someone whom another wants to undo; and a second time when He decides to destroy someone who is trying to improve his lot."

"Stop it, Salamat Bua," Chhami Begum would say. But the old

woman was deaf and cussed, and continued to mutter her ominous words.

It was a cold and misty winter morning. Chhami Begum had just finished taking her bath when Salamat's idiot daughter knocked on the door.

"Apa ... Apa ... come out ... hurry up ..." she shouted, jumping up and down.

"What is it, idiot?" Chhami Begum asked from inside as she wrapped a towel round her hair.

"Apa ... for God's sake ... the Master has come. He wants you to send him tea and hot pakoras."

Chhami Begum could not quite believe her ears. In the semidarkness of the bathroom, she frantically groped her way to the window, stood on tiptoe and peeped out of her "Shah Jahan's window." The courtyard had suddenly come to life. Servants bustled around. Suitcases and holdalls were being carried in. Somebody haggled with the driver of the horse carriage outside the entrance. And then her eyes fell on a woman! A dark, sour-faced slut in a red georgette sari. The next moment he came in ... handsomer than ever. He went up to the woman and said something. They laughed ...

Ali Baba's Cave turned into a deep dark well into which Chhami Begum fell headlong, feeling dizzy and suffocated as if in a nightmare. She swayed and fell, then passed out in a swoon.

Late in the evening, Ajju Bhai brought his wife inside. A little self-consciously, he came near the main door, cleared his throat and said: "I say, Chhami, come here. Meet your new relative."

Chhami Begum stood in the inner verandah. She trembled, felt dizzy again and shot back into the bathroom. She bolted the door from inside. In the verandah the couple stood around awkwardly for some minutes, then went back to their house.

Chhami Begum had come to know about the woman. She was shocked – not so much because Ajju Bhai had betrayed her and married someone else but because he had married a whore and brought disgrace to the family honour.

Ajju Bhai's wife tried to meet her again. She was formerly known as Miss Kallo Bai of Lucknow; Gramophone and Radio Singer. She desperately wanted to be accepted as the daughter, in-law of the family. But Chhami Begum had ordered the doorman, Dhammu Khan: "If you are a real Pathan, break the legs of anyone - man or woman who dares to enter my house!"

She began to wear white like a widow and became indifferent to worldly affairs. She let her relatives cheat her out of her remaining property. Ajju Bhai sensed the situation. He was stricken with guilt. He resolved to fight court cases on her behalf and sent her a large sum of money through an aunt. Chhami Begum was livid. She strode down to the gatehouse, from where her voice could be heard in the men's quarters, and declaimed: "Dhammu Khan, let it be known that I, daughter of Jumma Khan and niece of Shabbu Khan, would prefer to starve rather than accept any money touched by the inmates of brothels ..."

She had to sell her jewellery in order to run the large house and support hordes of retainers and good-for-nothing relatives. When the ornaments were gone, she opened a little school for the girls of the neighbourhood and took in sewing. The hangers-on left her. Only the two old faithfuls remained – Dhammu Khan and Salamat Bua.

Chham! Begum fell ill. The fever rose and she became delirious. Salamat panicked and sent for Ajju Bhai who called the family doctor. Ajju Bhai and his wife sat by her bedside and nursed her. When she opened her eyes, she saw the couple hovering over her. She gave Kallo Bai a withering look and closed her eyes again. Kallo was terrified of her husband's strange and imperious cousin. Quietly she crept back to her house.

Chhami Begum recovered.

It was the summer of 1947. There were Hindu-Muslim riots and talks of abolishing the zamindari system. Ajju Bhai, who had already run through most of his inheritance, went to Delhi to see a lawyer. There, one day in September, he was killed in a riot.

The day the news of his death came, Chhami Begum was fast asleep on her ottoman in the verandah. It was late afternoon. Kalla came running to the gatehouse and banged on the closed door. "Open the door!" she screamed hysterically. "Please open the door! A terrible thing has happened! We are ruined!"

Chhami Begum woke up with a start. The courtyard was as desolate as ever. The leaves of the tamarind rustled in the breeze. The scream pierced through her sleepy haze and hit her again. She got up and looked around. Kallo was pounding on the door with her fists. Chhami Begum took the key off a hook in the wall and ambled down to the entrance. Grumbling to herself, she opened the door.

There stood Kallo, her long hair spread over her shoulders. She looked terrible, like a black witch. Her face was contorted, she had injured her wrists trying to break her glass bangles against the door. For a few seconds she stared at her husband's haughty cousin. Then she lurched forward and tried to embrace her. Chhami Begum stepped back. Kallo broke into a long and loud wail: "Apa ... I have lost my kingdom ... My crown has fallen into the dust ... I have become a widow ... He is dead!"

Chhami Begum was still drugged with sleep. She rubbed her eyes and looked at the frenzied woman. Slowly, the truth dawned on her. Then she sat down on the threshold and covered her face with her white muslin dupatta. Her sobs mingled with Kallo's hysterical jabbering.

"Apa, I have become a widow ..." Kallo screamed again.

Chhami Begum wiped her tears and pulled herself together. She stood up, erect and imperious as ever. She said firmly: "Wretch! You have become a widow today, I have always been a widow. Go away, go back to where you belong!"

She slammed the door, bolted it from the inside and returned to her divan.

After a few days, Kallo disappeared – along with Ajju Bhai's costly belongings. Through the bathroom window Chhami Begum watched the woman pack up and leave with cartloads of expensive stuff carpets and paintings and silver and crockery. Chhami Begum did not feel anything. She merely watched, stony-eyed, another scene of the passing show ...

The Government Custodian put a seal on the adjoining house. Chhami Begum was unable to prove that Ajju Bhai had been killed in the riots and had not migrated to Pakistan. The house was declared Evacuee Property. Chhami Begum could not care less.

After a few weeks, a Sikh refugee doctor from Lahore and his family took up residence in Aziz's house. The Sardarni became friendly with Chhami Begum. Dhammu Khan died after a long illness. Salamat had become a cripple. Most of Chhami Begum's relatives and servants left for Pakistan.

The refugee doctor's daughter was married to a minor official in New Delhi. When the girl came to Shahjahanpur to visit her parents, she met Chhami Begum. The girl told her parents that her husband's Muslim boss was looking for a needy lady from a good family to teach Urdu to his children. The doctor's wife persuaded Chhami Begum to accept the position. "Behnji, how long can you live like this, all by yourself, with no income? Swallow your pride. There is no harm in working for one's living."

Chhami Begum agreed. It suddenly occurred to her that when she grew old and died, there must be someone by her bedside to read the Quran and perform the last rites.

So Chhami Begum packed a few clothes, put on her burqa and stepped out of the threshold of her forefathers' haveli which had now been reduced to a magnificent ruin. Zamindar Jumma Khan's daughter had become a genteel, impoverished teacher going out into a strange, unknown world.

Chhami Begum spent twelve long years in New Delhi with the Sabihuddins. They were good to her and treated her as one of the family. But their children grew up and Mr Sabihuddin retired and decided to go back to his hometown, Mirzapur. They passed Chhami Begum on to the Rashid Alis, with whom she spent five years as a housekeeper. The Rashid Alis also treated her well and called her Shams had khala, Aunt Shamshad.

Mr Rashid Ali was transferred to the Indian Embassy in Washington and did not know what to do with Aunt Shamshad. Was she to be left all alone once again?

One day Mrs Rashid Ali went to the Roshanara Club to attend a farewell lunch, and then went off to visit some relatives in old Delhi.

Chhami Begum arrived at the club and waited on the lawn. She always wore a white sari and looked like an upper-class ayah. As she walked up and down, waiting for her mistress, she saw a stylish lady staring at her from under a garden umbrella. She was playing cards with some equally stylish men. She was very beautiful and sophisticated almost like a model in a fashion magazine. Chhami Begum having lived for seventeen years in New Delhi had got accustomed to modem affluent women. She noticed the lady looking at her again. Soon a bearer came to her and said that the Memsaheb wanted to speak to her.

Chhami Begum went over to the bridge-table. The lady smiled and said that she was looking for a respectable but needy woman who could stay with her in Bombay as a sort of housekeeper. She had too many servants and really there was no work to do. She just wanted a motherly old woman around. Did she know anybody?

Chhami Begum whispered her thanks to the merciful God who closed one door but always opened another. She told the lady that she was about to be relieved of her present job and would she please speak to her mistress.

Mrs Rashid Ali arrived. The lady introduced herself as Razia Bano from Bombay and asked her about Chhami Begum. Razia Fano was flying to Bombay the next morning. Chhami Begum could follow by train whenever it was convenient. Mrs Rashid Ali looked relieved. But she asked Chhami Begum anxiously, "Khala, can you travel all alone to Bombay?"

Chhami Begum nodded. There was no longer any need in life to say "No". She did not even negotiate a salary. She had settled for forty rupees with food and did not need more. She did not mind wearing cast-off clothes. Long long ago she had realized that fancy clothes, ornaments, property, money, relationships, love and affection Were all meaningless, shadowy and transitory. Only Allah's Name Was Eternal, Everlasting.

From her huge bag, Razia Bano fished out one hundred and fifty rupees, along with her address. "Your fare to Bombay and for other expenses," she said casually. Mrs Rashid Ali was amazed. Chhami Begum remained nonchalant. She knew that Bombay was the city of tycoons. Life had ceased to surprise her anyway.

Alone at Bombay Central Station, Shamshad Begum got a little unnerved. The crowds scared her. She came out, clutching at her little paandan, then got into a taxi and gave the Sikh driver the address.

The taxi stopped at a gleaming block of flats on Warden Road. Chhami Begum stepped out. A Gurkha watchman sat stoically on his stool. She went into the foyer and was baffled by the automatic lift. "Beta," she called timidly, "how does this thing work?" A liftman materialized and took her up to the eleventh floor. He carried her luggage up to a double-leaved door and left. She rang the bell. Somebody peeped through the magic eye. Then the door opened. Another Gurkha came out and looked at her with suspicion. She became nervous again. She reminded herself that she was a brave Pathan. With great dignity she said: "Please tell the Begum Saheba that Shamshad Begum has arrived from Delhi."

"I know. Come in," he said curtly and opened the door. He picked up her little trunk and bedroll. She followed him, still clutching at her paandan and fan. They crossed a large drawing-room which had a bar at one end and a little cinema screen on a wall. Then they entered a gallery which had closed doors on either side. The Gurkha led her to a small, bare, servant's room and dumped the luggage on the floor.

"Is the Begum Saheba in?" Shams had asked politely.

"Yes. Sleeping."

"And Saheb."

The Gurkha did not answer and strode away.

The room was bare and stuffy. There was a small wooden bed with no mattress. "It will give me a backache," she thought simply, and opened the window.

She was confronted by a shimmering, blue-green sea. She had never seen the sea before. It fascinated her. Then, suddenly, it occurred to her that Mecca and Medina were right there, across these shining waters. "Allah in His great Goodness and Mercy, has brought me all the way to Bombay. Some day soon He will take me on the Haj pilgrimage as well." The thought brought tears to her eyes. She moved away from the window.

The flat was eerily quiet. She decided that the Saheb must be in his office, the children away at school. "Let me see if the Begum has got up from her siesta." She walked down to the end of the corridor and saw a half-open door. She knocked on it.

"Come in."

She entered a luxurious air-conditioned bedroom. Razia Bano lolled on a four-poster. She wore a fluffy peignoir and was smoking a cigarette. A white telephone and a golden notebook lay beside her on the silken eiderdown.

"So you have come, Bua. Sit down, sit down," she indicated the floor.

Shamshad Begum was taken aback. She had never been called a Bua. Only servant maids were called that. She had never sat on the floor. She pursed her lips and sat down on the edge of the sofa. She wanted tea. She did not approve of her new mistress's revealing dress and her smoking. But then she thought to herself: "Every place has its own customs. Such must be the custom of Bombay."

Razia Bano eyed her with amusement and said, "Bua, I am glad you have come. I did want someone like you - innocent and God-fearing. I can judge people, you know. I had guessed at once that you were a decent old woman. Now look, I must tell you a few things. You do not have to do any work. Just stay in your room and pray. I always want some elderly lady to stay in the house and recite the Holy Quran every morning and pray for my well-being. I had a pious old Hyderabadi lady who lived here. The poor thing died last year."

"We have two Goan ayahs to look after our wardrobes, etc. You may, once in a while, supervise the kitchen or prepare a special Mughlai dish or two."

A smartly dressed young girl with a cigarette in her mouth entered the room. Razia Bano said something to her in English. She giggled and went out.

"Your daughter? Masha Allah, how many children do you have?" Shams had Begum asked with sudden interest.

"My niece. I have no children."

"And your Saheb? Does he do business?" She had heard that everybody in Bombay did business.

"My husband is dead." Razia Bano replied curtly. Then went on: "So I was telling you ... Do not listen to gossip. Do not fraternize with the servants. Bombay is a terrible place. And these are evil times. All sorts of things happen here. Don't get shocked. Also, my nieces are modern girls. A lot of friends come to see them. You understand?"

She did not. But she nodded vaguely. Mr Sabihuddin's children also had a lot of school friends. She badly wanted some tea.

"I run a large business," Razia Bano continued. "Import-export. Various kinds of people come to see me about it. And being an enterprising woman, I also have many enemies. That is why I have had a steel door fixed outside. The police have raided us twice."

"The police?" Shamshad Begum repeated with alarm.

Razia Bano laughed. "Don't worry! The police often bother big business people like us. That's why, when someone rings the bell, be very careful ... "

Shamshad Begum yawned again.

"I will tell the bearer to give you some tea."

"Thank you," Shamshad Begum said, getting up, and returned to her room.

She said her afternoon and evening prayers and felt very bored.

There was nothing to do. The flat was silent again. She stirred out of the room when the front bell rang. She forgot the instructions of her mistress and rushed to the drawing room. Quickly she opened the door. Two men entered. One wore a silk kurta and a snow-white dhoti. There was a flash of diamonds on his fingers. He was very fat. The other was dressed like a film star. He was sleek and oily. Both flopped on a sofa and spread their legs.

"Bai ... Where is Madam?" the Seth asked.

Shamshad Begum was horrified. What kind of language was this? Where she came from only courtesans were called bai. Primly, she said: "Begum Saheba must be in her room. May I know your august names?"

"Forget our names! Call the chicks."

"Where are those girls?" the oily one asked.

"We were given this time."

Shamshad Begum couldn't quite understand what they were saying but their Urdu was certainly atrocious and she was about to tell them to mind their language and manners when Razia Bano came rushing in. She looked at Shamshad Begum and said: "Oh Bua, please go to your room and rest. Will you?"

"Yes, I will, thank you," Shams had Begum said simply and trotted back down the corridor.

The woman is senile, Razia Bano thought irritably and turned to greet the visitors.

Back in the little room, Shamshad Begum unrolled her prayer rug and sat, down to pray yet again. She thanked Allah who only laughs twice and Who, in His infinite wisdom and mercy, had given her shelter once more in a decent household and provided her with an honest livelihood.

SALIM AGHA QAZILBASH

THE UNIT

TRANSLATED BY ATANU BHATTACHARYA

$\mathcal{S}$alim Agha Qazilbash was born in 1956 in Lahore, and belongs to a family which has strong links with rural Pakistan. He obtained an MA in Urdu from Punjab University before returning to his rural homeland. Later, he received his PhD, again from Punjab University, in 1996. A noted short story writer, his stories are an authentic reflection Of the tradition and culture of a multi-tiered society gradually getting transformed through social and political upheavals. His published works include a collection of light essays, *Sargoshian* and two collections of short stories, *Angoor ki Bel* and *Subah Hone Tak*. Salim Agha Qazilbash lives in Sargodha, Pakistan.

"Ekai" was first published in the journal *Auraq*, Jan-Feb 1997.

This story has been translated here from a Devanagiri transcription.

$\mathcal{H}$e put his own life at stake in trying to save the drowning girl, but when he reached the banks of the river, carrying her body in his arms, she had already breathed her last.

He had been convicted of murder. No one had seen him rescue the girl. Everyone was convinced that he had drowned her because of some old malice he bore towards her. The sarpanchs of the kabila, after much deliberation, decided unanimously that he should have the freedom to choose between either getting his hands or feet cut off, or his eyes gouged out. He was told to make his choice. If he failed to do so by dawn, his head would be chopped off.

When they had gone away, leaving him incarcerated in the cell, he tried to regain his mental composure by taking a few deep breaths. He had to arrive at a momentous decision. One wrong step would lead him to annihilation, destruction. Suddenly, he felt his body going stiff. His heart started pounding deliriously against the prisonhouse of his ribs, as if wanting to shatter its walls and escape. He thought he sensed a dank mass quietly creeping towards him, from the various nooks and corners. Overcome with fatigue, he lay down on the reed mat, inert and lifeless.

But in a few moments he was sitting up again, rubbing his palms restlessly. Why had such a bizarre sentence been passed on him? The sarpanchs could have decided on the punishment once they had established his guilt. They probably want to murder me with my own hands! What a horrible way to wreak vengeance! This is treachery, an abhorrent conspiracy! He was beginning to realise for the first time how dreadful it is to have to choose a punishment for oneself.

His eyes were the first to see the girl drowning, and his feet had rushed to the banks of the river of their own accord. And then, his hands had reached out to grasp the drowning girl and carry her back to the shore. In other words, his eyes, hands and feet were all equally responsible for this act. But who had taken the lead? Surely not the eyes! Was it his feet? Or perhaps the hands? Who was responsible for this deed? Yes, it was definitely his eyes that had pushed him into the jaws of death.

But the eyes were helpless. They were mere witnesses to the incident. The wrong step had been taken by the feet for they had rushed into this mess.

No, the act had been really executed by the hands. Even if his eyes and feet had committed the crime in haste, the hands ought not to have collaborated. If they had halted in time, he would not have had to go through these moments of agony. But he did not have the time to think. He had received an order from somewhere within him and he had dived into the river in a flash to rescue the girl. Who had given the command?

Every passing moment and each heartbeat propelled him towards dawn. For the first time he despised the arrival of dawn. His heart screamed in agitation, pleading fervently for a thunderstorm that would overwhelm the world with its darkness and postpone the coming of dawn.

It was at the end of the first pahar of night that he resolved to allow them to have his feet severed. Relieved at having arrived at a decision, he was all of a sudden overcome by a tremendous thirst. But as he rose to drink from the dingy pitcher balanced on two bricks at the corner of the room, a wave of tingling pain started crawling upwards from the soles of his feet. It spread throughout his body, gradually engulfing it. His thirst disappeared.

He walked back to the reed mat and, sitting down, he began to stroke his feet lovingly. He turned breathless at even the thought of going through life without them, of having to rely on crutches to take even one step forward. A person who cannot stand on his feet is like a building that has been raised without a foundation. It is destined to crumble.

He was still wandering in the labyrinth of choices when the night crossed the mid-mark of the second pahar. In a rush, he resolved to get his hands severed. This decision conjured up for him the image of a man who tries to traverse the distance between the two ends of a taut rope without any balancing props. In the pit beneath, poisonous snakes were waiting to spit their venom and scorpions crawled, brandishing their stings. These creatures were leading a unified onslaught against him. He started extirpating the loathsome creatures from his body like a deranged man.

At that moment, he realized the grave implications of the decision to get his hands severed. He recoiled at the very thought of such a horrible prospect. How helpless and dependent a person becomes with his arms mutilated! Hands are the helm which enable the boat

Pahar: one-eight part of a day.

of existence to keep afloat in the torrential river of life. Without them it would be like rowing a rudderless boat. His hands were two sheets of paper on which his future life was inscribed. Without them, he would be at someone's mercy even for a single bite of roti or a drop of water. Such a life of largesse and dependency would reduce any man to a status more lowly than that of an earthworm.

The third pahar was coming to an end when he decided to let them gouge his eyes out. He had reached this decision after deep introspection. He thought he could somehow go through life groping with his hands; if he leaned on a stick he would be saved from falling into pits; or he could expend life's journey by holding on to someone else's hand. At least the outer framework of his body would be left unharmed. Eyes are anyway perpetually famished. All vices, desires, aspirations enter the heart through these windows. The light of the eyes can always be replaced by that of the heart.

Convinced by his own arguments, he closed his eyes, exhausted by the night-long vigil. Perhaps, he even dozed off. The twittering of birds startled the flaps of his eyes open. He stared vacantly at the empty wall in front of him for a few moments. When he regained his senses, he was overwhelmed by a desire to view the glory of daybreak. In almost a trance, he dragged his feet towards the lone window of the cell, and looked out, raising himself on his toes. The panorama was breathtaking. A sparkling festoon of white herons flew across his vision. His entire being gazed out through the window of his eyes. Moments later, a flock of birds soared from the dense foliage of a neem tree as if someone had flung a handful of glittering coins in the air.

And at that moment he realized that he would not be able to live without the colours of life. He could see the two burning rods approaching his eyes, he shrieked in terror. He sat down on the ground and, covering his eyes with his arms, started weeping bitterly. When his tears had stopped, he felt something creeping out of his body. He was in the clutches of an inexplicable shiver. He felt as if millions of ants were crawling all over his body and the thing that was leaving his body got stuck in his throat. His forehead was marked with beads of perspiration, the veins of his neck became taut and then his entire being went numb. At that very moment, someone forced open the colourless iron door of the cell. The door creaked as if in pain. The sound of heavy boots reverberated across the room. The brutal eyes of the perpetrators of justice saw a man crouched directly below the lone window of the cell. Hiding his eyes between his knees with his hands firmly round his legs, he sat on the damp stone floor like an immobile, insensible bundle – as if his limbs had been moulded in wax, forming a complete indivisible unit.

SURENDRA PRAKASH

BIJOOKA

TRANSLATED BY SARA RAI

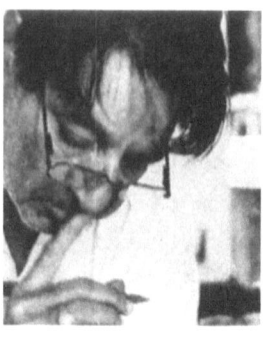

$\mathcal{S}$urendra Prakash was born at Lyallpur, now in Pakistan. He passed his school examination as a private candidate from Punjab University, Lahore, and published his first short story in Paras Weekly at a very young age. After Partition, he migrated to Delhi and made his living in a variety of ways – as hawker, rickshaw-puller, flower seller, and travelling salesman. He is at present involved in writing scripts for films and television serials.

Surendra Prakash is among the first few writers of the new short story in Urdu, which had its origin in the fifties. A majority of his works deal richly with the unexplored levels of mind and sensibility. Among his better-known works are *Doosre Aadmi ka Drawing Room* (1968), *Barf par Mukalma* (1980) and *Baz Goyi* (1988). He received the Sahitya Akademi Award in 1990. Surendra Prakash lives in Mumbai.

"Bijooka" is one of his well-known stories.

$\mathcal{H}$ori, of Premchand's story, had grown old. So old that his eyebrows and eyelashes were grey, his back was hunched over, and the veins on his hands stood out in a visible pattern on rough, dusky skin.

During this time, two sons had been born to him. But they were no longer alive. One had drowned while bathing in the Ganges. The other was killed in a police encounter. There is not much to tell about an encounter with the police. When one is at peace with one's inner self, but lives in the midst of restlessness, a confrontation with the police becomes inevitable.

Hori's sons had left behind their wives and their children, five in all – two born to the son who had drowned and three from the son killed in the police encounter. The burden of their upkeep had passed to Hori. Blood flowed with renewed vigour through his aging body.

Old Hori's hands, clutching the plough, relaxed for a moment. Then his grip tightened once more. He yelled out to his oxen, and the plough moved forward, rending the breast of the earth.

That morning, the sun had not yet risen. A rosy glow spread

across the sky. The five children were naked, bathing at the well in Hori's courtyard. The older bahu drew the water and poured it on the children in turn as they splashed around joyfully. The younger bahu was making huge rot is and carefully putting them away in a changri.

Inside the hut, Hori was already dressed and in the process of tying his turban. Having done that, he glanced at himself in the mirror placed in a niche in the wall. A face furrowed with lines looked back at him. Then he turned and stood in front of a picture of Hanumanji, his head bowed, eyes shut and hands folded. Coming out into the yard, he called out, "Is everyone ready?"

"Yes, Bapu!" they replied, in one voice. His bahus straightened the pallus of their saris, their hands beginning to move faster. It was quite obvious to Hori that no one was ready yet. We cannot live without lies, he thought. These lies are so vital for our existence. If God had not given us the gift of lies, we could not live. It all begins with a lie. The effort to pass the lie off as a truth keeps a man alive for years.

Hori's grandchildren and bahus set out to prove the truth of the untruth they had just uttered. Meanwhile, Hori was busy gathering the tools they would need for harvesting. By the time that was done, the others were, indeed, ready.

The rays of the sun cast a magical aura around their house. Their mood was festive. Today they would reap the harvest. Full of enthusiasm, they were impatient to reach the field, their green, golden field, swaying in the breeze.

These were good times indeed, thought Hori, settling the red-and-white checked angochha more comfortably on his shoulder. One did not have to put up with the bullying of the overseer or be wary of the bania, suffer the tyranny of the angrez or the greed of the zamindar.

Happiness burst like fireworks in their hearts as images of golden crops floated before their eyes.

"Come on, Bapu!" His eldest grandson took his hand, while the others latched on to his legs. The older bahu shut the door of the house. The younger one put the changri of rotis on her head.

Uttering the name of Bir Bajrang Bali, they trooped out into the lane.

The village was already bustling with activity. Groups of people could be seen moving towards their fields. Others were wending their way back to their village.

Life today was somehow different from yesterday. Or so Hori felt. He turned to glance at the children following him. What else could children of peasants look like? Dark and sickly, they would probably scurry away at the sound of a jeep. Even the changing seasons would alarm them. His bahus, too, were no different from the widows of other peasants. Faces obscured behind pall us, like the wretched lice lurking in the folds of their clothes.

Hori walked on, his head bent. From a distance, he and his family resembled insects of myriad hues, crawling in the dry grass.

Beyond the last house in the lane were the wide, open fields. The water wheel nearby stood still. A dog slept peacefully under a neem tree. Cattle, content after a meal, rested in their enciosures. The fields were a golden expanse in the distance.

Old Hori's land lay beyond these fields, across the canal. It stretched out languorously, waiting for him. Where Hori's field ended began a vast tract of barren land - parched land, with not a speck of green. Your feet would sink in if you tried to walk on that fallow, crumbling soil. The earth there easily turned to dust, just as the bones of his sons had turned into ash when they were cremated. Ash which scattered like sand at the merest touch.

The wasteland was gradually moving in, towards his field. Hori noticed that in the last fifty years it had advanced by two yards. He did not want it to swallow up his field before his grandchildren grew up. By that time, he too would have become dust. Just another part of some such barren land.

The path ahead seemed endless, but the bare feet of Hori and his family moved resolutely forward ...

The sun was peering over the eastern horizon. The long walk had made their feet dusty. Farmers, reaping the crop in the neighbouring fields, called out, "Ram-Ram!" and continued working with renewed zest, the golden stalks falling under scythes that moved rhythmically.

They crossed the canal, one by one. There was no sign of water, not even enough to create an illusion of it. The water that had once flowed through it had etched strange patterns in the dry sandy soil.

The golden field came into sight and their hearts lit up with joy.

Once the crop was cut, their yard would be full of hay, and the hut full of grain. What a pleasure it would be to sit on the charpai, gorging on rice! And how they would belch!

Suddenly Hori froze in his tracks. Those following him stopped too. Hori stared at the field, horrified. The others looked first at Hori, then at the land, trying to fathom what had happened. Something shot through Hori's body like a thunderbolt. He stumbled forward screaming. "Abbe, who is it ... ?"

Just then they noticed a strange movement in the middle of the waving field. They followed Hori with quick steps. Hori shouted again, "Abbe" who is that? Who's in my field? Say something, will you? Who is cutting my crop ... ?"

There was no reply. They were almost in the field now and could clearly hear the swish of the moving scythe. They stopped, a little unnerved. Tightening his grip on the scythe he held in his hand, Hori challenged, "Haraamzade, speak up!"

Slowly, an apparition was seen rising at the far end of the field. A figure that seemed to be smiling at them. And then they heard it speak.

"It's me, Hori Kaka ... me, the bijooka, the scarecrow!" it said, brandishing the sickle it held in its hand.

Stifled screams of fear escaped them. Colour fled their faces. Hori's parched lips turned white. They were stunned into silence. For how long? A moment, a century, an age? Who knows! They were lost to everything around them. The sound of Hori's rasping voice, quivering with rage, jolted them back to the present.

"You ... bijooka ... you! I made you from bits of straw to keep watch on my crops. I dressed you in the khaki clothes of the angrez shikari whom my father helped. The shikari had left them behind as a token of appreciation. I made your face with a pot, discarded from my house. I placed the angrezi hat on your head. And now, you lifeless puppet, you dare to reap my crop?"

Hori advanced as he spoke. The bijooka, not in the least perturbed by what Hori had just said, grinned at them. As they came closer, they saw that a fourth of the crop had already been harvested. And there the bijooka stood, smiling, sickle in hand. Where could it have got the sickle from, they wondered. Hadn't it been under their Watchful eyes all these months, standing there, lifeless, empty-handed? And today ... why, it could be a man! A flesh and blood person, no different from them!

The sight of it standing there, drove Hori out of his mind. He lunged forward and gave the bijooka a violent shove. It did not budge. But with the impact of the blow, Hori was hurled to the ground. Screaming, the people behind Hori ran up to him. He was struggling to rise, one hand supporting his back. They helped him up. He stared at the bijooka, a frightened look on his face, and said" So you have become stronger than me, bijooka! I, who made you with my own hands, to stand vigil over my crop."

Smiling as always, the bijooka spoke, "There is no need to be so upset, Hori Kaka. I have only taken my share of the crop ... one-fourth, that's all."

"Why? Who are you? What right do you have to a share at all?"

"I do have a claim to the crop, Hori Kaka. Because I am. I exist.

And because I have kept watch over this field."

"I put you there, knowing you had no life. How can a lifeless object have rights? Besides where did you get that?" Hori asked, pointing to the sickle.

The bijooka guffawed. "Hori Kaka ... you are talking to me and yet you insist I am lifeless!"

"But how did you get the sickle? And life? You had neither when I made you."

"Well, it happened on its own ... the day you split the bamboo to make my frame, dressed me in the angrez shikari's rags, etched eyes, nose, ears and mouth on a broken pot – even that day, life was seething in all these things. When they were put together, I came into being. Meanwhile the crop was ripening, and I stood there, biding my time. A sickle slowly began to take form within me. By the time the harvest was ready, so was the sickle – the sickle you see in my hands. However, I did not betray the trust you had placed in me. I waited patiently for this day. Now when you are ready to reap the harvest, I too have taken what is due to me. What is wrong with that?"

The bijooka spoke in a slow, deliberate manner. The import of its words was immediately clear to all of them.

"But this is impossible ... it's a conspiracy against me. As far as

I'm concerned, you are not alive. Don't think you can get away with this, you schemer! I'll go to the panchayat. Put that sickle down. I won't let you take a single stalk!" Hori yelled.

The bijooka flung the sickle away, the smile still fixed on its face.

The panchayat met in the chaupai. It was to take a decision that day. Both the concerned parties had already stated their claims. The sarpanch and the panch were present. Hori sat in their midst with his grandchildren. Signs of deep anguish were imprinted upon his pale face. His bahus stood with the other women. They were all waiting for the bijooka.

At last, they spotted the bijooka in the distance, ambling along.

Smiling, of course. All eyes were lifted towards it. There was something about its appearance that commanded respect. As it entered the square, everyone stood up. Involuntarily, they bowed their heads. The sight disturbed Hori. He couldn't ignore the niggling feeling that the villagers had allowed their conscience to be bought by the bijooka. So had the panchayat, it seemed. He felt helpless, desperate – like a drowning man wildly thrashing his limbs.

The sarpanch announced the verdict. A tremor went through Hori as he agreed to give the bijooka a fourth of his crop. Then he rose to his feet and addressed his grandsons.

"Listen. This is probably the last harvest I will live to reap. The arid land hasn't reached our field yet. My advice to you is this, never set up a bijooka to guard your crop. When the field is ploughed next year and the seeds are sown, and the nectar of rain brings forth new shoots, bind me to a pole and stand me up in the field instead of a bijooka. I will look after your crops till your fields are swallowed by the arid waste and the soil turns to dust. Don't ever remove me. Let me stand testimony to the fact that you did not make a bijooka. A bijooka is not lifeless as it is supposed to be. Indeed, it acquires a life of its own. And this fact of existence itself invests it with a sickle. To say nothing, of course, of its right to a fourth of the harvest."

Having said this, Hori trudged towards his field. His grandchildren walked behind him, followed by the two bahus. Then came the villagers, with slow unhurried steps, their heads drooping low.

They had almost made it to the field when Hori collapsed. His grandchildren immediately set themselves to the task of tying him to a pole, under the curious eyes of the spectators. The bijooka took off the shikari's hat, held it against its chest and bowed its head.

SYED MUHAMMAD ASHRAF

AADMI

TRANSLATED BY SALEEM KIDWAI

Syed Muhammad Ashraf was born in 1957 in Sitapur. He received his primary education in Marhara Sharif in Etah district, Uttar Pradesh. He has an MA from Aligarh Muslim University. A gold medallist at both his BA and MA examinations, he serves as Deputy Commissioner, Income Tax, in the Indian Revenue Service. Syed Muhammad Ashraf is essentially a short story writer. His collection of Urdu stories Daar se Bichde was published in 1994. He also has to his credit critical works on the Urdu short story. His novel *Numbardar ka Neela* was published recently. His works have been translated into Hindi and English. This story "Aadmi" won the Katha Award for Creative Fiction in 1995. Syed Muhammad Ashraf lives in Mumbai.

"Aadmi" was first published in *Daar Se Bichhre,* October 1994, Bombay.

$\mathcal{H}$e stood there watching them pass below his window. Then, abruptly, he closed the window with a bang, turned and pressed the fan's switch – now on, now off – before leaning against a chair near the table.

"Their numbers increase every day," he said softly.

Sarfaraz raised his head from his open palms to look at him.

"You've only seen it for two days. I've been watching this for weeks. If I keep the window shut, I feel suffocated. If I open it, it gets worse. All of them seem to be heading this way." He fell silent for a moment. Then, "I'm meeting you after such a long time," he said.

"I feel so happy. Yet ... these people ... "

"I've told you what happened on my way here. And it isn't as if I've just noticed it. Back in the village it's the same. I can't say what this might lead to."

Sarfaraz looked at his childhood friend with affection. He was meeting Anwaar after fifteen years. How many memories they shared! As a boy, Sarfaraz had been sent to his uncle's home to study. Khalu lived in a large village. Two miles away, in the qasbah, was an

Inter College. On his first day there, a boy of about his own age had casually taken Sarfaraz's eraser to rub out the balloon-like flowers he had drawn in his copy. Replacing them with a duck which looked like a lamp, he had returned the eraser. During roll call the teacher had called out, "Sayyid Anwaar Ali?" and that boy had said. "Haazir Janaab."

"Sayyid Anwaar Ali," Sarfaraz muttered.

"Haazir Janaab. Thinking of school, are you?"

"Yes. How did you guess?"

"Yaar, you still speak like a villager. Only the Drawing Masa'ab during roll call ever called me by my full name."

Sarfaraz smiled. He did not like being called a simpleton. But then, he reasoned, he was a senior officer and this childhood friend of his, an Urdu teacher in a primary school. He calls me names because he feels inferior, Sarfaraz told himself, and this thought made him feel better.

It was at that same moment that his mind leaped back in time – but for Anwaar, he would have never been able to get home from school, not one day! Without Anwaar, he would have been half-dead with fear by the time he crossed the dark jungles, the deserted orchards, and the silent fields that lay between the qasbah and the village.

Sarfaraz rested his head on the back of the chair and closed his eyes. How pleasurable it was to remember that childhood terror!

In early winter, classes ended at four. When the last bell rang, a chattering crowd rushed out of the classrooms, bags on shoulders, feet dancing homeward. He was the only one from his village, in this college. He would leave the college gates with slow, hesitant steps, afraid of the terrifying journey home. Sometimes Anwaar would be with him, walking up to the lake - but even he would not go beyond that. The road turned sharply at that point and if you looked back from there, the qasbah had disappeared. Before going his way, Anwaar would reassure him. "Don't be scared, Sarfaraz," he'd say always. "Once you cross the canal and enter the grove, you'll find someone there."

Feeling helpless, but too embarrassed to show his fear, Sarfaraz would put on a brave face. "What is there to be afraid of? Sometimes I meet someone in the orchard and that's good, but even if I don't, it doesn't worry me." With an air of nonchalance, he would head for the village, but he remembered how both of them would keep turning to look at each other.

The moment Anwaar disappeared from sight, Sarfaraz would touch the taweez around his neck and quickly start reciting the ayt-al-kursi. Before reaching the canal he would have also chanted the four quls and blessed himself. Praying each step of the way, he would then move towards the grove. It was usually dark - the sun set early in winter.

On the dirt track, before he turned onto the narrow path by the canal, a solitary cyclist or a bullock-cart would occasionally pass by, bells tinkling. But once he reached the embankment, it was totally deserted. The eerie sound of a vulture shifting perches high above on the shisham or rearranging its rustling wings made the desolation even more frightening. He would not be able to recall the ayt-al-kursi sometimes, and would start reciting the qul-o-wallah-o-ahad instead. Sometimes he even managed to repeat the first kalima, the kalima-i-tayyib.

The grove would then appear, its aging mango trees shrouded in the mist of fading day. One Sunday, he discovered that it was perpetual dusk inside the grove, even at midday. In the evening, of course, it became darker. It was as if the tips of trees had crowded together in a conspiracy. Passing under the fajri tree he would hear his heart pound. It would seem as if Jinnaat Baba would, that very instant, descend from the tree.

After the grove lay the sugarcane fields. Walking past them, he was certain that at any moment a lurking wolf would spring out from the fields to grab his leg. Palms sweating, he would hurry into the wheat fields which came next. At last, over the pilkhan trees, the minars of the masjids and the kalash of the village temples would appear. His body would relax, strength slowly returning to his legs. And he would break raucously into a film song.

Once or twice a month, when entering the grove he would see a man walking towards his hut, a spade in his hand. On those days, a relieved Sarfaraz would start singing in the grove itself, breaking off only to wish the man – with great familiarity. The man would put down his spade when he heard Sarfaraz's loud, "Salaam huzoor!" He would squint at him and say, "Ram-Ram, beta. Aren't you Patwari sahab's nephew? My greetings to him." Not that he met the man every day. But it was the hope of meeting him that gave Sarfaraz the courage to return home from college. Otherwise, he would have given up his studies and returned to his own village.

One day it was late by the time he left college. He had been so engrossed in watching a volleyball match that he did not realize the time. When he looked up, the sun had turned red. He set out in a hurry.

As he turned on to the path along the canal, he shuddered at the thought of not seeing the man on the way. He wiped the sweat off his forehead as he walked past the shisham tree. Suddenly he was sure someone had slid down the branches and was following him. His mouth went dry, he could not breathe. With slow, scared steps he moved on. Then the sounds behind him stopped. Maybe Jinnaat Baba was taking aim now to shoot a magic ball at him. Feverishly reciting the kalima, he peered over his shoulder. It was a large monkey on all fours, growling at him. He was afraid of monkeys too, but not as much as he was of Jinnaat Baba. Clutching his bag, he hurried on. His pace slackened only at the edge of the grove. Ahead was the deserted grove where he had no hope of finding the man this late. Behind him was the monkey.

The sun had set quite a while ago. The trees of the grove had begun their evening whisperings. He entered the grove. Walking towards the old fajri tree his heart beat fast. This was the real abode of Jinnaat Baba ...

Then he heard a voice. "You are very late today, beta."

Arre, the man was there after all! Sarfaraz was more pleased to see him than he was when the English teacher had given him a Very Good for writing "My Cow."

He looked at the man. He was standing among the trees near his hut. He was leaning on his spade, one hand resting on it, the other pulling his angochha over his ears. Wrapped in mist, the man in an ordinary dhoti, kurta and angochha looked like an assistant of Hazrat Khizr, the prophet who had drunk the waters of immortality.

"Salaam," Sarfaraz said happily. "Salaam huzoor!'"

"May you live long, beta. Say Ram-Ram to Patwari sahab. And try not to be so late."

That night, Sarfaraz ate his dinner and then went and sat with his aunt in the dalaan. Impulsively, he hugged her and told her the whole story. He wanted his khala and khalu to know what he had to brave every day to attend college. But when she heard that he had got late because of a volleyball match, Khala was furious.

Snuggled into his razai, he lay in the dalaan, worrying how he would ever return from school if the man were to die. But the man looked younger than Khalu. Surely, he was unlikely to die soon! Anwaar's voice broke in on his memories.

"Your cousin is getting married," Anwaar was saying. "Your khala called to complain that you have totally forgotten them. She said I should tell you that they are eager to see you. And that you must attend the wedding."

Sarfaraz felt contrite, but he did not want to show it. In a grave but hollow voice he told Anwaar that one found little spare time when working for the government, especially as he was in a responsible position. Then he remembered Ayesha. He used to play with her when she was a baby. How quickly she had grown up!

"When is the wedding?"

"The baraat arrives the day after tomorrow."

"Arre! Why has Khala gone and fixed a date now? Hasn't she seen the madness all around? Hordes of people, their faces blazing red, are out there in their trucks and tractors. They always carry weapons and there's such hatred in their eyes ..."

"Yes, I did tell Khala that this is not the time for celebrations. Every village has been infected by the madness. Attitudes have changed in her village too, but she has no choice. The boy they have chosen for Ayesha is Khalu's brother's son. He is returning to Jeddah in three days. Besides, Khalu has not been too well. He is anxious to see Ayesha settled. You must leave at once, Sarfaraz. Ring up Bhabhi and tell her to get ready."

"Don't you read the newspapers, Anwaar? Just the day before yesterday, people were dragged off a train and ..."

Anwaar too was silent. Then he said in a brisk voice, "Achha then, leave Bhabhi and the children here."

"Yes, I won't be able to take them along."

"It is eleven o'clock now. Even if we start at twelve, we should reach by seven, before it gets too dark."

"Yes. It's about two hundred and fifty kilometres, right?"

They were on the bridge across the canal when some people suddenly stepped in front of the car and motioned them to stop. A procession of trucks and tractors was coming their way. The crowd was shouting frenzied slogans and seemed driven by a strange passion.

Sarfaraz's heart sank. They were carrying no weapons, nothing to defend themselves with. They sat still in the car. Sarfaraz found himself silently repeating the ayt-al-kursi.

The procession went past them. The people who had stopped the car started shouting slogans and as the procession moved on, they joined it, still shouting.

Sarfaraz sat frozen, unable to start the car. Anwaar sat quietly beside him, each instinctively aware of the other's fear. When finally he started the car, Anwaar said, "I have always found that they never do anything to individuals on open roads. For that they have trained people in each village and town. Last Friday when Ahmad the shopkeeper turned on to the path by the grove, someone came from behind him and ... "

A chill ran down Sarfaraz's spine. He drove on mindlessly, as Anwaar continued to talk. "It wouldn't look good if a crowd were to attack isolated people. But then, we are well prepared too," he added in a conspiratorial whisper.

Finally when they turned along the canal road, the sun was already setting. How terrifying these places had seemed once, this silent canal, the deserted path and the whispering groves, Sarfaraz thought. Had it not been for that man with the spade ...

He braked suddenly. Caught in the headlights of the car was a huge monkey, its palms resting on the ground, making the growling sound he remembered so well.

They smiled as they watched the monkey run up a tree. In the branches, a vulture moved. A sound of fluttering wings. How that sound used to scare me, thought Sarfaraz.

"When was Ahmad attacked?"

"Four days ago."

"Arre ... Sarfaraz's hands that gripped the steering wheel were damp with sweat.

"What's up?" Anwaar asked, though he knew what the matter was.

"Nothing. So the incident was recent. Did they find anything?"

"What could they find? Right after the burial, the thanedaar scolded us for letting people walk through the grove alone after sunset in times like these. Attackers find it easy to operate at night. Stop, Sarfaraz. The road ends here, remember?"

They got out of the car. They walked past the embankment.

Sarfaraz was stepping into the mist-shrouded grove after a long time. Today it held no fear, yet a strange quiet had entered both of them. It didn't go away even when they spoke loudly to one another.

And then, as they passed the ancient fajri tree, Jinnaat Baba's haunt, Sarfaraz suddenly clutched Anwaar's hand so hard that Anwaar almost cried out in pain.

He looked at Sarfaraz, who was staring at a large mound. In the dark Anwaar could not even make out what Sarfaraz was pointing to.

Sarfaraz squeezed his hand harder. Then, abruptly, he turned around and ran, dragging Anwaar along and, stumbling ... slipping ... scrambling up, they rushed out of the grove. Sarfaraz pulled the car door open, pushed Anwaar in and drove off at full speed.

Soon they were speeding across the bridge and on to the familiar dirt track.

A nerve twitched in Sarfaraz's cheek. He was bathed in sweat. "Tell me," said Anwaar finally. "Whatever it was, we have left it behind. Tell me what happened?"

Sarfaraz stopped the car.

"There was that man standing on the mound in the grove, among the trees. Did you see what he had in his hand, the thing on which he was leaning? It was a ... rifle."

⇁ UMRAO TARIQ ⇀

THE LAST STATION

TRANSLATED BY ANUPAM PRABHALA KAPSE AND P L NARASHIMHAM

𝒰mrao Tariq is the pen name of Syed Umrao Ali. He was born in 1932 at Fatehpur Haswa, a small town in Uttar Pradesh, India, and received his early education in Allahabad and Kanpur. After migrating to Pakistan, he obtained an MA in Political Science and a degree in Law.

He served as a Deputy Superintendent of Police and was Principal of the Police Training College. He is currently associated with Anjuman-e-Taraqqi-e-Urdu, as its Joint Secretary. His first collection of short stories, *Badan ka Tawaf* (1979), won the Adamji Literary Prize. His other published works include *Khushki par Jaziray* (1986), *Dhanak ke Baqimanda Rang* (1993). His most recent work is *Ma'tub*, a nove1.Umrao Tariq lives in Karachi.

"Aakhri Station" was first published in the special annual issue of *Sareer*, 1996.

$\mathcal{N}$obody knew what station it was. The stationmaster's room was locked. The window of the ticket counter was shut, as sightless as a blind eye. The shelterless platform was empty. Signboards bearing the name of the station were covered with so much soot that the letters on them were completely blacked out. The signal cabin was deserted, and the levers used for changing the tracks pointed upwards, like guns trained on the sky. There was not a soul around. The third class waiting room, open on three sides, also lay abandoned. Not a dog, not an animal, not even one crawling insect was visible. No birds on the horizon, not even a sparrow in the sky.

Outside the station, the road too was deserted. Loose gravel lay scattered over the road, waiting to be crushed by the heavy road roller. On the other side of the road, the railway staff quarters were silent, the tattered jute curtains over the doors of some houses swaying in the breeze, revealing black and yellow locks on the doors.

In the train, the passengers sat as if petrified ...

In just a little while the sun would set.

The train was heading north. It had four passenger bogies, some

207

dusty, red coloured wagons, followed by another bogie for passengers. At the time of its departure, the train had been empty. But the terrain it had to traverse was so steep that the train had two coal-fed engines, one at each end. Negotiating the last gradient, passing the outer signal first, then the south cabin, it came to a stop on the outer line away from the platform, as if expecting another train from the opposite direction.

An epidemic had broken out. The disease had spread all over, beyond the station, to the neighbouring villages and towns. People were dying. Slanting lines, the municipality's symbol of death, crisscrossed the front walls adjoining the doors of houses where the disease had sneaked in.

When the train had reached the station, more than half the houses bore these marks beside their entrances. At first, everybody had said that the situation would soon be brought under control, that there was no need to abandon the village and the houses. The question of evacuation did not arise. But when the pestilence reached their neighbourhood and bodies piled up, one on top of the other, the people began to flee.

After the Asr ki Namaz, the shabrati, the jolaha, ramzani tamkhalan, hafiz aatishbaaz, and the Maulana Sadan had sat with bowed heads on the parapet of the big mosque. Fear flickered on their faces like the shadow of a neem tree. Each one would comfort the other, but deep inside their hearts, terror grew.

It was a weekly bazaar day when the District Commissioner came to reassure tlle villagers. People from nearby villages also joined the gathering. They were all looking at the Commissioner as if their saviour had come to rescue them from this horror. The Commissioner had with him the thanedar, a police platoon, and a retinue of orderlies in attendance. A brief speech was made, assurance given that the situation would remain under control, there was no need to run.

The thanedar kept nodding his head in agreement, but looked around with frightened eyes as if somebody was about to leap out from the gali nearby and plunge a khanjar into his stomach.

The Commissioner made his speech and went away.

A number of people died that night.

The teli climbed the low mud wall opposite the small mosque and shouted:

"Shabrati oh Shabrati!"

"Yes, Aatishbaaz!"

"Ramzani Tamkhalan!"

"Hafiz ji!"

"We have been betrayed!"

When the train arrived at the station the shabrati, ramzani, hafiz aatishbaaz and the Maulana Sadan were present on the platform along with the villagers. They jumped into the first bogie they saw. A few weary travellers were sitting inside. Very soon it was full. Some forced their way into the bogie next to the front engine.

"Go to the back! There is no space in this bogie, there's no water!"

The distressed passengers started getting into the second bogie.

"Go back! Don't force yourselves into this compartment – there's no water here ... "

The desperate passengers dashed towards the third bogie.

"Go back! Two bogies are empty back there, and there are goods wagons too ... Climb on to them!"

The shabrati, thejolaha, ramzani tamkhalan, hafiz aatishbaaz, and Maulana Sadan: The devout, the weavers, the ramzan fasters, the fire-blowers, and the religious head.

teli: oil-maker

"Travelling on a goods wagon is a crime, it is not allowed."

"Nothing is unlawful now. If you think about all that you'll miss the train."

Most of the passengers hurriedly boarded the very last bogie as the train started to move. Those who were left out clambered on to the roofless goods wagon.

The two engines started pulling and pushing the train towards its final destination. All five bogies and the wagons were crammed with people. The climb was tough, the ride slow, but the travellers were determined, satisfied and happy.

But after many sleepless nights passed, the passengers stopped caring about the others. They sat, their legs stretched out, quite oblivious of the fact that, in their sleep, their feet poked into the faces of their fellow passengers. Little by little, those who were strong succeeded in making space to tuck their kith and kin in with them. They were also storing the water in the bogie, in their own utensils.

Tension mounted in the last bogie. Because of the shortage of space and water in the front compartments people were getting off at small, little known stations and getting into the fourth and fifth bogies - not through the doors but through the windows, squeezing themselves in, treading upon the passengers inside. The inside was getting cramped. The atmosphere changed. Passengers in the fifth bogie shut fast the doors, pulled down the window shutters, piled their belongings against the doors and sat firmly upon them. People from the front bogies continued to climb into the fifth one. Kicking and screaming, they tried to force the windows open, leading to quarrels, big and small. The train kept moving.

One morning, just after daybreak, they saw that the fifth bogie and the rear engine were no longer connected to the train. Only four bogies and the goods wagon remained. The fifth bogie and the rear engine were nowhere to be seen. Not even in the far distance.

There was widespread speculation in the train.

"They've run away quietly, with their engine and bogie ... "

"Maybe dacoits attacked them and captured their engine and bogie ..."

"Perhaps the driver of our front engine detached their bogie sometime in the middle of the night and brought the rest of the train ... "

"That's impossible!"

"Why not?"

"How can it happen?"

"You don't know, the people in the front bogies must be in league with their driver ... "

"Is such a conspiracy possible without anybody's knowledge?"

"Everything is possible ..."

From the goods wagon, which had no roof, a man shouted.

"We've been betrayed!"

And everyone recalled Basanta teli who had shouted the same message to them from the top of the wall across the small masjid.

A night of helplessness crept silently into the desolate station. The compartments were overflowing with men, women and children. Suckling infants stuck to their mothers' chests like leeches. Fear had dried up their milk. Terrified, the children fell to the floor of the bogies, their mouths still searching. The men cocked up their ears, trying to catch the sound of new dangers. The slightest rustle would make them jump, like rabbits. They had neither weapons nor ingenuity nor vision to protect themselves and their children.

The people packed into the wagons began to feel the chill of the icy wind that started blowing as soon as the sun had set. The plight of the children was getting worse. They huddled under their mothers' dupattas, shivering and clinging, like the British holding on to Hind; and at the same time there was an onslaught of mosquitoes drinking away the blood even as it flowed over the border.

On one side of them, stretching to the horizon spread the sands of the desert, rising and flooding their mouths and eyes, while on the other side lay a dense jungle from which a wild beast might emerge to make a meal of them all.

The village they had left behind, its security, the sweet cold water of its wells, kept haunting their memories and they sobbed. Grief and repentance stood before them. All night, hunger, thirst, terror and discomfort kept them awake but in the small hours of the morning the passengers in the goods wagons fell asleep. When they opened their eyes at daybreak, the four passenger-filled bogies with the closed doors and windows and the engine had vanished, leaving the open wagon friendless and helpless.

And now, on this desolate station without water or plant, there was no bogie, no engine, and no compartment except these roofless wagons on the far side of the platform. Who knew where and when in the dark of the night the front engine had disappeared taking away the bogies with windows, doors, roofs, water, and the passengers who filled them.

The men, women, old folk and children loaded into the roofless wagons stared at each other, bewildered. All around, deep into the far distance, neither an animal nor a bird could be seen.

Not even a sparrow in the sky.

⌒ ZAHEDA HINA ⌒

MIRAGE ON WATERS

TRANSLATED BY RASHMI GOVIND AND AYESHA SULTANA

Zaheda Hina was born on 5 October, 1946, in the historical city of Sasaram, Bihar. She has been involved with literature and journalism from the age of sixteen. Her collections of short stories include *Quidi Saans Leta Hai* and *Rah Mein Ajal Hai*. Her well-known work *Na Junoon Raha Na Pari Rahi*, is a sensitive portrayal of the partition of the subcontinent. Zaheda Hina has been translated into Hindi, English, Gujarati, Marathi and Bangla by various translators including Faiz Ahmed Faiz and Amrita Pritam, and her stories have been included in Urdu and English anthologies. For the last ten years she has been a regular columnist for the Sindi journals *Rozana Jung, Jadda, Ibrat* and the weekly, *Zindagi*. She has served the BBC Urdu Service, Voice of America and Radio Pakistan. Zaheda Hina lives in Karachi.

"Paaniyon Mein Saraab" first appeared in *Qaidi Saans Leta Hai*, 1983.

$\mathcal{I}$ read the words *Ismat Panah* on the heaqstone of the grave and couldn't help laughing. I said to Azfar, "You must have *Protector of Chastity* inscribed on my gravestone too."

Azfar smiled blankly as we walked out, past the graves. The car started, and Ahsan began to talk about the term Ismat Panah. Soon the discussion veered to the different points of view about chastity and the parameters of chastity at different periods of history: Shahriyar of Alif Laila; the unfaithful princesses and the Negro slaves who had access to their privacy; the streets and alleys of Baghdad; the palaces and the gardens of Naples and Florence; Pompeina, Ninette and Madeleine of *Decameron* – lovers who wore their hearts on their sleeves, and damsels who opened the doors of their bedrooms as soon as their husbands' backs were turned.

I tried changing the subject but one viewpoint led to another till we finally reached the question whether the concept of chastity and purity was subjective, or not. Jokes and anecdotes were exchanged and someone referred to chastity belts.

Ahsan narrated the story of a Christian crusader who, before departing for battle, made his wife wear a chastity belt. He should have taken the key with him. But he was a man with a sense of justice and he gave the key to his friend so that, in case he died in the war it could be handed over to his wife, allowing her to marry anyone she desired. The soldier had gone only a short distance when his friend came galloping behind him, panting, "You have given me a wrong key by mistake. This is not the key to your wife's chastity belt."

And then someone else started on another story. A princess whose beloved husband was going to war decided to wear a chastity belt and to throw the key into a pond, in the presence of her husband. Soon a day came when she fell in love with another man. And she spent all her wealth in hiring divers to retrieve the lost key!

We continued to exchange stories till we reached Kanjhar Lake.

Golden sunshine shimmered on the green molten glass-like waters. At the bottom of the clear lake, lush green moss tangled with water plants that swayed with the waves. A flock of water birds came flapping down and skimmed to a stop. The boat moved forward, the shore receded, and the trees, the people sitting in their shades and the huge trucks which were being carefully washed, all faded into mere shadows with the growing distance.

There was a sound behind me and I turned round. The fish that Azfar had caught near the shore, was lashing about on the floor of the boat. "Please Azfar, throw it back into the water," I cried out in distress. "What? I have managed to catch one with such difficulty, and you want me to throw it back? You really are something!" A streak of pleasure lit up Azfar's eyes as he watched the fish writhe. I glanced at Yusuf who was sitting opposite me. He lowered his eyes.

Safia Ahsan opened the thermos and started pouring coffee into the mugs. For want of something to do, I began to help her. The samosas had turned cold but they tasted good with the hot coffee.

Coffee is meant to be enjoyed sip by sip; samosas are to be savoured bit by bit; and I exist so that, by day the torture of separation can turn me to water; and at night, the vulture of my husband's, my earthly god's, carnal pleasure can devour me, piece by piece. This coffee is better off than me. It is drunk at once and that's the end of it. Even the samosa is chewed, swallowed and it's finished. Each night devours me, and yet my existence doesn't end. Each day consumes me, and I continue to exist.

Ahsan started to hum as he drank his coffee ... *Akele mat jaiyo Radhe Jamuna ke teer.*

I looked at him with trepidation. How do you know the secrets of the heart? Isn't only God supposed to know them? And who knows whether He exists or not in the role of the omniscient?

Ahsan's voice rose on the waters, spiralling like a whirlwind. *Akele mat jaiyo Radhe, Akele mat jaiyo Radhe ... O Radha, don't go alone to the banks of the Jamuna.*

The water of Kanjhar Lake began to recede, it flowed into the depths of the earth, the deep green water of the Jamuna getting diffused over the pupil of my eye, plumbing its depths, stretching over a wide expanse, *"Akele mat jaiyo Radhe ..."*

But I had not gone anywhere alone. Azfar had left me on my own. He was to be away for just two days. He rang up to say that he would have to be in Bombay for two more days. His business trip would be a waste if he didn't meet some important people there.

Yusuf, and I roamed around Delhi during this time. I spent the time complaining to Yusuf about Azfar's inattentiveness towards me and he gave me a patient hearing. I told him that money was not everything. Love was as important as companionship. Azfar had no time for things such as a wife, children, relatives. The real issue was money and more money.

My intellectual voyage began in dreams and ended in books. Money can buy books but dreams are not sold in a market, they cannot be bought, can they? What then was I to do with so much money? Even as our future grew more and more secure, I wondered where it left me. How could I account for the wasted moments of my life? Yusuf and Azfar were childhood friends. In spite of the differences in their natures, they met whenever they could. Like his father, Azfar had gone into business and made his fortune. Yusuf was a dreamer right from the beginning. He dreamt of palaces and mansions, of castles and labyrinths. He became an architect, a man who could transform heaps of cement, gravel, stone, lime, steel and aluminium into dreams for people to live in. He was an international celebrity. His creations were scattered across America, the Continent and the Far East.

When I spent some time with Yusuf in London, I discovered a new side to his personality. This man who could create a variety of buildings out of crude things was a poet at heart. When intoxicated he would hold forth on the art of architecture. He once said that the construction of a building was in reality the metamorphosis of matter.

Yusuf was a great admirer of the Gothic style of building and of cathedrals. According to him, their altars, their corridors, their confessionals, all reflected the depths of the human soul, its repentance and its closeness to Jesus Christ. He would say that every great building is a metaphor of its times and unless one internalized this metaphor" one would not be able to appreciate the beauty and the mysteries of the building.

One evening he was at my flat, having a drink and talking. Whenever he had a few pegs he became eloquent. The poet in him would come alive, and beautiful ideas would start flowing. That night he was talking about Borromini, Bernini, Alberti and Michelangelo. He considered these famous artists his spiritual mentors and he said that he would give anything for an apse or a column from a building created by them.

It was during this conversation that somehow I started talking about seeing these ancient buildings and ruins by moonlight. He burst out: "What nonsense! It is only silly, romantic women and foolish men who talk of seeing Roman ruins by moonlight or the cathedral in Paris at night. Let me tell you that apart from the Shalimar Gardens and the Taj Mahal there are only a handful of buildings that are meant to be seen by moonlight. Castles, palaces and mansions, all the great buildings of the world were built to be seen and used during daytime. The slanting rays of the morning or the afternoon sun accentuate the grandeur of these buildings, illuminate the beauty of each wall and define the curvature of each dome. Night robs most buildings of their beauty, hides the sharpness of their contours. A building which appears attractive only by moonlight cannot be included in the list of great buildings."

He liked to discuss the economics and the sociology of buildings. How much was spent on a particular building. Where the money came from. On whom the taxes were imposed, and how strict was the collection. Were the men who constructed the building free labourers, or helpless bonded slaves. Were the people who made these buildings innovative, or did they follow the beaten track. Did the labourers sing while they worked, or did the air resound with the crack of whips on their backs.

When he discussed politics with reference to architecture, his views became complicated and distasteful, and then we got into useless and heated discussions. He would say that most of the great buildings of the world owed their existence to the decisions and desires of despotic kings and that architecture cannot flourish in a democracy.

Yusuf took me to see all the great buildings in London. When he spoke of columns, arches, apses, entrances, of doors and gateways, when he explained the interplay of light and shade, when he explained the subtle differences made by the blowing of the breeze and the advent of sunlight according to the changing seasons, I would feel as if these desolate buildings were alive once more, as if the sunlight had just that moment climbed down from the ramparts and entered the heart of the fort where Henry VIII was turning over in his bed to gulp down his first draught of the day.

Yusuf had a wonderful knack for friendship. He was Azfar's friend but whenever I met him I felt as if he was my friend and mine alone. Genuine, truthful, he understood my pain. If I did not meet him for some time I would feel a pang in my heart. If I did not receive his letter I would be anxious and write to him – How are you? Where are you? Why have you not written for so long? And then he would send a long reply containing information about all kinds of things. Azfar and I would derive a lot of pleasure reading his letter.

Azfar and I were about to leave for India, when suddenly Yusuf arrived one evening. He had come to stay with us for some time - to rest, he said, relax. When he came to know that we were going to India, he decided to accompany us. The three of us arrived in Delhi, and as usual, Azfar left me in the hotel and went to Bombay, caught as usual in a web of material pursuits.

Yusuf and I were left alone to roam the galis of Delhi. Forts, mosques, shrines, gateways, bawlis, we visited them all. There was no desolate spot that we did not haunt. We went to the banks of the Jamuna, descended the steps of the ghat and sat side by side. The hot midday sun shone down on us. All around us there was silence, quietness. Perhaps it is at such moments that the spirit of Khuda moves on the waters.

I leaned forward to touch the water, the essence of life. When I turned my head to say something to Yusuf, I saw him looking at me, and there was a world of meaning in his eyes. We stood naked in front of each other with all our inner curses and blessings, in all our folly and repentance, like Adam and Eve when they tasted the fruit of the tree of knowledge and suddenly discovered that they were unclad. We were no longer two persons, separate. For a long time now we had been deluding ourselves in the name of friendship and companionship. That one moment changed everything. It was a strange moment, a moment when one learnt the lesson of love.

Suddenly the boat lurched. The raasleela which had filled the eyes disappeared. The waters of the Jamuna vanished in the twinkling of an eye. We were on the flowing waters of Kanjhar Lake. Yusuf stood poised in his yellow swimming trunks in the front portion of the boat - there was a splash and his golden body entered the green waters of the lake. He swam alongside our boat, spraying us, disappearing into the water and then reappearing. Looking at his naked body I felt as if I was born from his rib, as if we were a single body, the first couple on earth. I lowered my eyes. I was scared that Azfar would read on my face what was inscribed in my heart.

In the distance the earth and the sky embraced each other. A mere illusion, that. There were tears in my eyes. The two of us were that rim of the horizon. And when the illusion was broken, we were only earth and sky, destined never to meet. I was the earth, solid, fixed in my place. And he was the sky, mere empty space, an illusion. I was a woman, weak, unprivileged. I could go to any extreme for him. Yusuf was a man, courageous, bold, and so, unable to do anything. What would people say! What would happen to the children! What would be the effect on Azfar! Yusuf had travelled all the continents of the world. He had amassed a large fortune. He had become an international celebrity. But he still remained in the clutches of his middle class morality. He could share his friend's wife without the friend's knowledge. But he could not even think of confessing to Azfar the state of our desire for each other and then leave the resolution to him. I knew what Azfar's decision would be. Even Yusuf knew it. But then Yusuf had his values: Plain hypocrisy, simple dissimulation.

And now I spend my life between two men. Azfar, whose earth does not belong to him, who has had his house burgled. And Yusuf, who fears to free his land from the possession of others, and the revenue of whose land is deposited in someone else's treasury. *Talf hai murgha kibila numa aashian me.* Yes, the bird in the nest quivers, directionless, like a weather cock.

"Mrs. Azfar, do you know where you are at the moment?" Ahsan was asking in a dramatic fashion.

"What do you mean?" I looked at Ahsan a bit surprised. He was the manager of Azfar's London office and was visiting Karachi with his wife.

"You are passing over the shrine of Noori-Jam Tamachi."

"Why are you speaking in riddles?" Azfar was listening to us now.

"Azfar Saheb, we are indeed passing over the shrine of Noori-Jam Tamachi," Ahsan said. "As you know, this is the monsoon season and the level of the lake has risen. That is why the two shrines are under water. Otherwise, one can see the dilapidated shrines atop a small island. The local people even claim that on moonlit nights they can see Noori rowing on the lake."

"What are you people discussing? Why, only recently my wife

was paying homage at the shrines of Mikli, and I had to virtually drag her away from there. And now you have started talking about shrines all over again." Azfar made a sour face. "And look at Yusuf, diving into the water with such earnestness as if he were searching for something." He raised his voice and called out to Yusuf. "Head back, yaar! You are diving in vain, no princess has thrown the key to her chastity belt here."

Yusuf smiled at this remark and headed back towards the boat. Ahsan started laughing too. "Yusuf Saheb must be having quite a collection of such keys."

"This friend of mine, he is a deep one, he is – does not allow anyone to get even a whiff of these things," Azfar said.

Yusuf had climbed into the boat, the drops of water trickling down his body forming a puddle at his feet. The fish lying there was dead by now. Sophia Ahsan raised her eyes, glanced at us with indifference and then busied herself with her sketch book. Her greatest drawback was her reticence, her biggest achievement, her talent for painting. An exhibition of her paintings was to be held in Sydney in a few weeks.

I leaned over and looked at the water, water which is the flow of mystery; water, which is an expanse of fear and awe; water, which is the quintessence of life. The Rig Veda says:

"At that time there was neither nothingness nor existence, neither earth nor the sky, other than this. What was it that surrounded all? And where was it all? Was it not water, and an endless depth?"

This water on whose surface we were moving was not an endless depth, out it was water still, water, where desire appeared for the first time, desire, which was the original seed of the mind and soul.

Desire, mind, soul, love ... I was caught in a snare of all four. A cloud provided shade to our boat and moved with us. Perhaps we were actually passing over the shrine of Noori-Jam Tamachi. I wondered how the world must have been, centuries ago, when the shore of Kanjhar was inhabited by fishermen and when Jam Tamachi, the headman of the clan of Simma, lost his heart to Noori, a fisherwoman from the same village.

These two, who once used to wake up together, had now been sleeping side by side for centuries, and with them slept who knows how many kisses, consummated or otherwise; how many embraces, gratified or otherwise. I was reminded of Shah's Sur ka Mood. This raagini, said to be related to Deepak raag, sings the complete story of the star-crossed love of Noori-Jam Tamachi. Shah's voice wafted down –

Dhan daulat janta me bante, maya jal ko toda,
Kanjhar ki gandari ke karan raj pat ko chhora.

The one who had abdicated his throne and the fisherwoman of Kanjhar were sleeping in the depths of the lake, but it was Ghalib who had desired a burial by water: *Huye kyun na gharkdariya, na kahin mazar hota.*

The shrines of Mikli appeared in front of my eyes. The canopies shading the fourteenth-century graves, the turquoise and deep blue tiles shining like glass, the walls black with moss. This was the shrine of Mirza Khan Baba, the son of Mirza Khan Eesa Khan Turkhan the First. Here lie Malik Rajpal and Ahinsa Bai, Mirza Baqi Baig Uzbek, Mirza Tughral Baig. No one knows where they came from. They now lie here, row after row. Turk, Rajput, Mughal, Uzbek, Arghoon

---

Dhan daulat ... He severed all bonds of human desires and gave away all his wealth to the common people/He even gave up his throne for the fisherwoman of Kanjhar.

Huye kyun nagharkdariya ... Why didn't I drown in the depths of the river, No tomb would have been needed then.

– friend, enemy, father, sons, kinsmen and outsiders, all mingled with the dust, turned to dust. The Earth hides all secrets in her bosom like a mother the faults of her children.

As I passed by them, I paused to read the inscription on one of the tombs. I drew back in amazement. Engraved on the headstone were the words:

Ismat Panah Jahan Begum expired on the sixth day of the month of Zilhijjah, the year one thousand and eighty-two of Hijri.

At that moment it suddenly struck me how the words Ismat Panah would look on my headstone! That is why I had laughed and said to Azfar: "You must have *Ismat Panah* inscribed on my headstone too."

When Azfar instructed the boatman to turn back, we were in the middle of Kanjhar. We were going back on the very same waters over which we had travelled forward.

I often wish to go back in time, but it is not possible to take a journey backwards. I am tempted to ask Yusuf how much longer can he hide the fact that it is he who has the key to the chastity belt. I want to be a woman who belongs to just one man.

The boat is moving towards the shore, but I cannot do so. I have to remain in the middle of the waters, waiting for the day when even Yusuf loses the key.

As for Azfar, he lost it long ago.

THE TRANSLATORS

Anupama Prabhala Kapse has an M Phil from the University of Delhi and teaches English at Gargi College. She has been associated with Katha as a Telugu language resource person and as a translator for *Katha Prize Stories*.

Atanu Bhattacharya is a senior research student of English literature from Jawaharlal Nehru University, New Delhi. He teaches English at a college in Arunachal Pradesh.

Ayesha Sultana has obtained a Firdausi Gold Medal in MA Persian and a PhD in Urdu. In 1994 her PhD thesis on Urdu Short Stories was published. She has also done Certificate and Diploma Courses in Modern Arabic. At present she teaches at Zakir Husain College.

Gillian Wright is a well-known translator. She has translated two Hindi novels into English: *Raag Darbari* by Shrilal Shukla, *Aadha Gaon* by Rahi Masoom Raza. Professionally, a television and radio producer, she is also a writer of travel books.

Krishna Paul taught English literature at Jamia Millia Islamia, Delhi for many years. She retired recently and has been involved in translating short stories from Urdu and Hindi into English. Her translations have been published, in India and abroad.

Naghma Zafir teaches English at Zakir Husain College, Delhi, and has worked for the United States Information Services, as a translator. She has translated fiction and critical writings from Urdu, some of which have been published in *Urdu Canada*, *Urdu Alive* and *Kavi Bharati*.

Neshat Quaiser teaches in the Department of Sociology, Jamia Millia Islamia, Delhi. His doctoral thesis from JNU deals with nationalism, religion and peasant politics in the subcontinent. He is currently engaged in research work on diasporic memories and colonial experiences. He has written short stories in Urdu and poems in Urdu and English. His two translations included in this volume are dedicated to Sasha Nadira Jonaki.

P L Narasimham has an ME from the Indian Institute of Science, Bangalore. He was a Colombo Plan Fellow at Imperial College, London. At present he is a senior executive at Howe India Pvt. Ltd.

Rashid studied Persian in Jawaharlal Nehru University, New Delhi and is at present studying there in the School of International Studies, for his Master's degree.

Rashmi Govind has degrees in English and Linguistics from the University of Delhi and Jawaharlal Nehru University. She teaches literature at Zakir Husain College, Delhi. She has translated Abdul Bismillah's Hindi novel *Jhini Jhini Kali Badariya* into English (1997, Macmillan India.)

Saleem Kidwai retired as a Reader in History from Delhi University. He has published essays in journals and books in India. Founder member of the Conservation Society, Delhi, he has been a consultant to the Government of India for the Festivals of India in Great Britain and France, and for Apna Utsav.

Sara Rai is the editor of *The Golden Waist-Chain*, a selection of Hindi stories, and *Ababeel ki Uraan*. Her stories, articles and reviews have been published in leading journals and newspapers. She has received the award for translation for Urdu in the First Katha All India Translation Contest (1994) and the Katha Award for Translation (1996).

Shobhana Bhattacharji teaches English at Jesus and Mary College, University of Delhi. In her own words, she "loves the fabulous use of language, whether English or Hindi."

Tahira Khan, a poet in Urdu and in English is a postgraduate in English from Aligarh University. Her poems and stories have been published in Pakistan in *Mah-e-Nau*, *Naquoosh* and *Khartoon-e-Mashriq*. She has taught at Bombay and Gujarat Universities for twelve years. She has been translating literary works between English and Urdu.

THE ARTISTS

Nalini Malani, born in 1946 in Karachi, obtained her diploma in Fine Arts at JJ School of Arts, Mumbai, and was awarded a scholarship for further study in Paris. Apart from watercolour and oil on canvas, Malani has worked in diverse media like reverse paintings on Mylar, neon and video. She has also collaborated with theatre artists.

Risham Syed has an MA from the Royal College of Art, London. She has exhibited her work in galleries in England, Hong Kong and at Lahore and Islamabad, among other places. At present, she lives and works in Lahore, Pakistan.

Sheba Chhachi, born in 1958 in Ethiopia and educated in Delhi, Calcutta and Ahmedabad, combines the skills of a photographer, sculptor, writer and graphic designer. Since 1993, she has been working with multimedia installations and has created works articulating the history, experience and power of feminine consciousness.

Sylvat Aziz studied art in Pakistan and later in Montreal and Banff, Canada. She has exhibited extensively in solo and group shows, among the most recent of which are Muqqadimah (University of Calgary, Alberta) and An Intelligent Rebellion (Bradford). She lives and works in Canada.

THE EDITORS

Muhammad Ali Siddiqui, a PhD in Pakistan Studies, is a well-known literary critic and academician. He lives in Karachi and is at present the Director of Quaid-e-Azam Academy of the Pakistan Government's Federal Ministry of Culture.

For several years he lectured at the Pakistan Studies Centre, University of Karachi. He has been a literary columnist for Dawn for nearly 28 years writing under the pen name of Ariel and has been associated with the editing of *Pakistan and Gulf Economist, Daily Hurriyat* and *Brtish Review*. Some of his important publications are: *Tawazun* (1976), *Croce ki Sargozasht* (1976), *Nishanat* (1981), *Mazameen* (1991), *Isharye* (1994) and *Zikr-e-Quaid-e-Azam* (ed, 1996) and *Common Heritage* (OUP, Karachi, 1997). In 1976 and 1979, Siddiqui chosen for the Pakistan Writers' Guild Award and in 1995 he received the Baba-e-Urdu Award for literature.

Sukrita Paul Kumar was born and brought up in Kenya, East Africa. At present she lives in Delhi and teaches literature at Zakir Husain College, University of Delhi. She also supervises a project at Katha on translation studies and the academia.

As Fellow of the Indian Institute of Advanced Study, Shimla for three years, she worked on Hindi and Urdu short fiction. Her publication are: *Conversations on Modernism* (1990), *The New Story* (1991) and *Breakthrough* (ed, 1992). Her earlier book, *Man, Woman and Androgyny*, is a study of 20th century American fiction. Three collections of poems *Oscillations* (1987), *Apurna* (1989) and *Folds of Silence* (1996) of hers have been published. A recipient of Rockefeller Grant and Shastri Indo-Canadian Research Fellowship, she has lectured at various Canadian and American Universities. In 1994, her visit to Cambridge University was sponsored by the British Council and Charles Wallace Trust.

ḏb

STRMNG TO BUILD BRIDGES
BETWEEN LITERACY AND LITERATURE
KATHA PRESENTS

Exciting books at affordable prices!

"Katha is literally a literary institutions." – *India Today*

For Literary Connoisseurs

Katha Prize Stories 1-5	Rs 350
Katha Prize Stories 6-9	Rs 350
Katha Prize Stories 10-13	Rs 350

edited by Geeta Dharmarajan and Meenakshi Sharma
" ... an excellent series"   – Amitav Ghosh in *The Indian Express*

A Southern Harvest edited by Githa Hariharan   Rs 120
A collection of sixteen evocative stories from contemporary short fiction in Kannada, Malayalam, Tamil and Telugu.
" ... showcases the best of regional talents."   – *Business Standard*
" ... illustrates that fiction in South India is in a healthy state"
                                        – *World Literature Today* (USA)

Visions-Revisions 1 edited by Keerti Ramachandra   Rs 120
Award winning translations of twelve stories by master story tellers.
"The stories ... bring us the magic that is India."   – *The Pioneer*
" ... immensely earthy and Indian"   – *The Financial Times*
Visions-Revisions 2 edited by Keerti Ramachandra   Rs 120

Masti edited by Ramachandra Sharma   Rs 300
First in the Katha Classics series on great writers who have made landmark contributions to Indian literature.
"Masterly Rendition."   – *The Review of Books*
"Katha Classics are designed to endure"   – *Biblio*
Basheer edited by Vanajam Ravindran   Rs. 300
... lively stories ... a book well worth possessing"   – *Business Standard*
Mauni edited by Lakshmi Holmstrom   Rs. 300
"The most sensitively edited and translated Indian book ... a dazzling collaboration of love."   – *Indian Review of Books*

The Wordsmiths edited by Meenakshi Sharma   Rs 195
Interviews with five of the most exciting writers of our times, along with an alluring selection from their writing, fiction and nonfiction.
"... studded with gems from writers who are known for their excellence."
                                        – *The Hindu*

For the Young Adult

Yuvakatha 1-4 edited by Geeta Dharmarajan	Rs 30 each
Yuvakatha 5-8 edited by Keerti Ramachandra	Rs 30 each
"Heady tales."	*- Biblio*
A Unique Odyssey: The Story of the United Nations	Rs 120
by Geeta Dharmarajan, illustrated by Atanu Roy	
(Sponsored by the Rajiv Gandhi Foundation)	
"An exciting fusion of reality and fantasy."	*– The Asian Age*

For Children

Tamasha!   Subscription Rs 90 (for 2 years)
India's only development quarterly with stories, games and activities for children In Hindi and English.

Swapnasundari and the Magical Birds of Mithila	Rs 30
by Geeta Dharmarajan	
A JALDI fantasy in Hindi and English.	
The Secrets of Kalindi by Geeta Dharmarajan	Rs 50
A JALDI jigsaw puzzle adventure.	

For Neo-literates

Stree Katha	Rs 90
by Geeta Dharmarajan and Sheeba Chowdhary	
An information-packed, interactive volume on women's issues.	
" ... imaginative and approachable."	*– The Indian Express*

The **Katha Vachak Series:** Adaptations of classic Indian stories. In Hindi.

Stree ka Patra by Rabindranath Tagore	Rs 50
Paro ki Kahani by Sughra Mehdi	Rs 50
Puraskar by Jaishankar Prasad	Rs 50
Thakavat by Gurbachan Singh Bhullar	Rs 50
Faisla by Mqitreyi Pushpa	Rs 50
Faisla by Mqitreyi Pushpa	Rs 50
Bhola by Rajendra Singh Bedi	Rs 50
Samudra Tat Par by O V Vijayan	Rs 50
Sparsh by Jaywant Dalvi	Rs 50
Abhishap by Puduvai Ra Rajani	Rs 50
Panch Parmeshwar by Premchand	Rs 50
Do Haath by Ismat Chughtai	Rs 50

 *Special Offer*

15% discount for Friends of Katha on all books!
For a postage-free delivery, send a DD/MO made
out to KATHA at A-3. Sarvodaya Enclave,
Aurobindo Marg. New Delhi 110 017

ABOUT KATHA

Katha is a registered nonprofit organization working in the area of creative communication for development. Katha's main objective is to spread the love of books and the joy of reading amongst children and adults, with activities spanning literacy and literature.

Kalpavriksham, Katha's Centre for Sustainable Learning, develops and publishes quality material for neo-literate children and adults, and works with teachers to help them make their teaching more creative. It also publishes learning packages for first-generation schoolgoers and adult neo-literates. Specially designed for use in nonformal education, every quarter, Katha brings out *Tamasha!*, a fun and activity magazine on development issues for children, in Hindi and English. The *Katha Vachak* series is an attempt to take fiction to neo-literates, especially women. *Stree Katha* and *Stree Shakti* are illustrated, information-packed, interactive books on women's issues in a number of Indian languages.

Katha-Khazana, a part of Kalpavriksham, was started in Govindpuri, in one of Delhi's largest slum clusters, in 1990. Kathashala and the Katha School of Entrepreneurship have over 1000 students – mostly working children. To enhance their futures, an ihcome-generation programme for the women of this community – Shakti-Khazana – and the Khazana Women's Cooperative were also started there, again in 1990.

Katha Vilasam, the Story Research and Resource Centre, seeks to foster and applaud quality fiction from the regional languages and take it to a wider readership through translations. The Katha Awards, instituted in 1990, are given annually to the best short fiction published in various languages that year, and for translations of these stories. Through projects like the Translation Contests, it attempts to build a bank of sensitive translators. Katha Vilas am also works with academia to associate students in translation-related activities. It is working, specially through KathaSouth, to develop syllabi and teaching material for courses in translations. Katha has also been conducting workshops for teaching and reading translations in schools and colleges all over the country as part of the Kanchi Project, launched this year. Soon to be released are books in the Approaches to Literature in Translation series, which aims to provide texts for courses in translation. KathaNet, an invaluable network of Friends of Katha, is the mainstay of all Katha Vilasam efforts. Katha Vilasam publications also include exciting books in the Yuvakatha and Balkatha series, for young adults and children respectively.

alini Malani – 'Razai cover' – *Excavated images to stain an old quilt cover,*
Brought by my grandmother from Karachi in 1947

Risham Syed 1997

Untitle